The Blessing Way

The first book in award-winning Tony Hillerman's Leaphorn & Chee series, *The Blessing Way* follows Navajo Tribal Police Lieutenant Joe Leaphorn down a path of murder and mysticism as he tries to solve the homicide of a young boy whose only suspect is an elusive Wolf-Witch. Set against the rugged expanse of New Mexico's deserts, this mystery has thrilled and enthralled readers of crime fiction for nearly forty years.

HARPER PERENNIAL OLIVE EDITIONS

This book is part of a special series from Harper Perennial called Olive Editions—exclusive small-format editions of some of our bestselling and celebrated titles, featuring beautiful and unique hand-drawn cover illustrations. All Olive Editions are available for a limited time only.

The Blessing Way

BOOKS BY TONY HILLERMAN

FICTION

The Shape Shifter	*Skeleton Man*
The Sinister Pig	*The Wailing Wind*
Hunting Badger	*The First Eagle*
The Fallen Man	*Finding Moon*
Sacred Clowns	*Coyote Waits*
Talking God	*A Thief of Time*
Skinwalkers	*The Ghostway*
The Dark Wind	*People of Darkness*
Listening Woman	*Dance Hall of the Dead*
The Fly on the Wall	*The Mysterious West*

The Boy Who Made Dragonfly (for children)
Buster Mesquite's Cowboy Band (for children)

NONFICTION

Seldom Disappointed
Hillerman Country
The Great Taos Bank Robbery
Rio Grande
New Mexico
The Spell of New Mexico
Indian Country
Talking Mysteries (with Ernie Bulow)
Kilroy Was There
A New Omnibus of Crime

The Blessing Way

A Leaphorn & Chee Novel

Tony Hillerman

FIRST HARPER PERENNIAL OLIVE EDITION PUBLISHED 2019.

ISBN 978-0-06-295559-3 (Olive edition)

19 20 21 22 23 LSC 10 9 8 7 6 5 4 3 2 1

Acknowledgment

While ethnological material as used in this book is not intended to meet scholarly and scientific standards, the author wishes to acknowledge information derived from publications of Willard W. Hill, Leland C. Wyman, Mary C. Wheelwright, Father Berard Haile, Clyde Kluckhohn, and Washington Matthews; and the advice and information provided by his own friends among the Navajo people.

The Blessing Way

1

Luis Horseman leaned the flat stone very carefully against the piñon twig, adjusted its balance exactly and then cautiously withdrew his hand. The twig bent, but held. Horseman rocked back on his heels and surveyed the deadfall. He should have put a little more blood on the twig, he thought, but it might be enough. He had placed this one just right, with the twig at the edge of the kangaroo rat's trail. The least nibble and the stone would fall. He reached into his shirt front, pulled out a leather pouch, extracted an odd-shaped lump of turquoise, and placed it on the ground in front of him. Then he started to sing:

> *"The Sky it talks about it.*
> *The Talking God One he tells about it.*

The Darkness to Be One knows about it.
The Talking God is with me.
With the Talking God I kill the male game."

There was another part of the song, but Horseman couldn't remember it. He sat very still, thinking. Something about the Black God, but he couldn't think how it went. The Black God didn't have anything to do with game, but his uncle had said you have to put it in about him to make the chant come out right. He stared at the turquoise bear. It said nothing. He glanced at his watch. It was almost six. By the time he got back to the rimrock it would be late enough to make a little fire, dark enough to hide the smoke. Now he must finish this.

"The dark horn of the bica,
No matter who would do evil to me,
The evil shall not harm me.
The dark horn is a shield of beaten buckskin."

Horseman chanted in a barely audible voice, just loud enough to be heard in the minds of the animals.

"That evil which the Ye-i turned toward me
cannot reach me through the dark horn,
through the shield the bica carries.

It brings me harmony with the male game.
It makes the male game hear my heartbeat.
From four directions they trot toward me.
They step and turn their sides toward me.

"So my arrow misses bone when I shoot.
The death of male game comes toward me.
The blood of male game will wash my body.
The male game will obey my thoughts."

He replaced the turquoise bear in the medicine pouch and rose stiffly to his feet. He was pretty sure that wasn't the right song. It was for deer, he thought. To make the deer come out where you could shoot them. But maybe the kangaroo rats would hear it, too. He looked carefully across the plateau, searching the foreground first, then the mid-distance, finally the great green slopes of the Lukachukai Mountains, which rose to the east. Then he moved away from the shelter of the stunted juniper and walked rapidly northwestward, moving silently and keeping to the bottom of the shallow arroyos when he could. He walked gracefully and silently. Suddenly he stopped. The corner of his eye had caught motion on the floor of the Kam Bimghi Valley. Far below him and a dozen miles to the west, a puff of dust was suddenly visible against a formation of weathered red rocks. It might

be a dust devil, kicked up by one of the Hard Flint
Boys playing their tricks on the Wind Children. But it
was windless now. The stillness of late afternoon had
settled over the eroded waste below him.

Must have been a truck, Horseman thought, and
the feeling of dread returned. He moved cautiously
out of the wash behind a screen of piñons and stood
motionless, examining the landscape below him. Far
to the west, Bearer of the Sun had moved down the
sky and was outlining in brilliant white the form of a
thunderhead over Hoskininie Mesa. The plateau where
Horseman stood was in its shadow but the slanting
sunlight still lit the expanse of the Kam Bimghi. There
was no dust by the red rocks now, and Horseman wondered if his eyes had tricked him. Then he saw it again.
A puff of dust moving slowly across the valley floor. A
truck, Horseman thought, or a car. It would be on that
track that came across the slick rocks and branched out
toward Horse Fell and Many Ruins Canyon, and now
to Tall Poles Butte where the radar station was. It must
be a truck, or a jeep. That track wasn't much even in
good weather. Horseman watched intently. In a minute
he could tell. And if it turned toward Many Ruins Canyon, he would move east across the plateau and up into
the Lukachukais. And that would mean being hungry.

The dust disappeared as the vehicle dropped into
one of the mazes of arroyos which cut the valley

into a crazy quilt of erosion. Then he saw it again and promptly lost it where the track wound to the west of Natani Tso, the great flat-topped lava butte which dominated the north end of the valley. Almost five minutes passed before he saw the dust again.

"Ho," Horseman said, and relaxed. The truck had turned toward Tall Poles. It would be the Army people who watched the radar place. He moved away from the tree, trotting now. He was hungry and there was a porcupine to singe, clean, and roast before he would eat.

Luis Horseman had chosen this camp with care. Here the plateau was cut by one of the hundred nameless canyons which drained into the depth of Many Ruins Canyon. Along the rim, the plateau's granite cap, its sandstone support eroded away, had fractured under its own weight. Some of these great blocks of stone had crashed into the canyon bottom, leaving behind room-sized gaps in the rimrock. Others had merely tilted and slid. Behind one of these, Horseman knelt over his fire. It was a small fire, built in the extreme corner of the natural enclosure. With nothing overhead to reflect its light, it would have been visible only to one standing on the parapet, looking down. Now its flickering light gave the face of Luis Horseman a reddish cast. It was a young face, thin and sensitive, with large black eyes and a sullen mouth. The forehead was high, partly hidden by a red cloth band knotted at the back, and the nose was curved and thin. Hawklike. He sat crosslegged on the hump of sand drifted into the enclosure from the plateau floor above. The only sound was the hissing of grease cooking from the strip of porcupine flesh he held over the flame. The animal had been a yearling, and small, and he ate about two-thirds of it. He sprinkled sand on the fire and put the remainder of the meat on the embers to be eaten in the morning. Then he lay back in the darkness. The moon would rise sometime after midnight, but now there were only the stars overhead. For the first time in three days, Luis Horseman felt entirely safe. As he relaxed, he felt an aching weariness. He would sleep in a little while, but first he had to think.

Tomorrow, if he could, he would build a sweat house and take a bath. He would have to get a Singer somehow when it was safe and have a Blessing Way held for him, but that would have to wait. A sweat bath would have to do for now. It would take time, but tomorrow he would have time. He had what was left of the porcupine and he would have kangaroo rats. He was sure of that. He put out twelve or thirteen deadfalls baited with blood and porcupine fat and he thought the chant had been about right. Not exactly, but probably close enough. He would not think beyond tomorrow. Not now. By then they would know he had not gone back down to the Tsay-Begi country, to the clan of his in-laws, and they would be looking for him here.

Horseman felt the dread again, and wished suddenly that he had his boots and something that would hold water. It was a long climb down into the canyon to the seep. They would be looking anywhere there was water and even if he covered his tracks, there would be a sign—broken grass at least. The porcupine stomach would hold a little water, enough for a day. He would use that until he could find something or kill something bigger. But there was nothing he could do about his feet. They hurt now, from all day walking in town shoes, and the shoes wouldn't last if he had to cover much country.

Then Horseman became aware of the sound, faint at first and then gradually louder. It was unmistakable. A truck. No. Two trucks. Driving in low gear. A long way off to the west. The light night breeze shifted slightly and the sound was gone. And when it blew faintly again from the west, he could barely hear the motors. Finally he could hear nothing. Only the call of the nighthawk hunting across the plateau and the crickets chirping down by the seep. Must have been in Many Ruins Canyon, Horseman thought. It sounded like they were going down the canyon, away from him. But why? And who would it be? None of his clan would be in the canyon. His Red Forehead people stayed away from it, stayed clear of the Anasazi Houses. The Ye-i and the Horned Monster had eaten the Anasazi long ago—before the Monster Slayer came. But the ghosts of the Old People were there in the great rock hogans under the cliffs and his people stayed away. That was one of the reasons he had come here. Not too close to the Houses of the Enemy Dead, but close enough so the Blue Policeman wouldn't think to look.

Horseman felt his knife in his pocket pressing painfully against his hip. He shifted his weight, took it out, opened the long blade and laid it across his chest. Soon the moon rose over the plateau, and lit the figure of a thin young man sleeping, barefoot, on a hump of drifted sand.

Horseman was at the seep a little after daylight. He drank thirstily from the pool under the rock and then cleaned the porcupine stomach sac thoroughly with sand, rinsed it, knotted the tube to the intestine and filled it with water. It held about two cups. The sweat bath would have to wait. He couldn't risk building the sweat house here. And, if he built it in the protection of his camp, he had nothing large enough to carry water to pour on the rocks after he had heated them. He erased his tracks thoroughly with a brush of rabbit brush, and kept to the rocks on the long climb back to the canyon rim.

Four of his deadfalls had been sprung but he found dead kangaroo rats under only two of the stones. Another yielded a wood mouse, which he threw away in disgust, and the other was empty. He glumly reset the traps. Two rats were not enough. There were frogs around the seep, but killing frogs would make you a cripple. He would try for the prairie dogs. A grown one would make a meal.

The place Horseman had seen the prairie-dog colony was about a mile to the east. He used thirty minutes covering the distance, remembering the sound of the truck motors and moving cautiously. Maybe another of those rockets had fallen. He remembered the first time that had happened. It was the year he was initiated and there had been Army all over. Trucks and jeeps and helicopters flying around the valley, and they had come around to all the hogans and said there would be $10,000 paid to anyone who found it. But nobody ever did. Then they cut that road up Tall Poles and built the radar place and when the next rocket fell a year ago they had found it in two or three days.

He stopped by a dead juniper, broke off a crooked limb and started whittling a throwing stick. He could sometimes hit a rabbit with one, but usually not prairie dogs. They were too careful. While he shaped the stick he stared out across the Kam Bimghi. Nothing at all was moving now, and that probably meant it wasn't a rocket down. There would be a lot going on now if it was that. Besides, they wouldn't have been hunting a rocket at night.

He didn't have a chance to use the throwing stick. The burrows of the colony were bunched below a hummock of piñon and one of the rodents saw him long before he was in range. There was a chittering outburst of warning calls, and in a second the dogs were in their holes.

Horseman put the throwing stick in his hip pocket and broke a smaller limb from a piñon. He sharpened one end, split the other. Back at the prairie-dog colony, Horseman selected a hole which faced the west. He stuck the stick in the ground in front of it, pulled a thin sheet of mica from his medicine pouch, and slipped it into the split. He adjusted the mica carefully so that it reflected the light from the rising sun down the hole.

Now he could only wait. In time the light would attract one of the curious prairie dogs. It would come out of its hole blinded by the reflected sun. And he would be close enough to use the stick. He glanced around for a place to stand. And then he saw the Navajo Wolf.

He had heard nothing. But the man was standing not fifty feet away, watching him silently. He was a big man with his wolf skin draped across his shoulders. The forepaws hung limply down the front of his black shirt and the empty skull of the beast was pushed back on his forehead, its snout pointing upward.

The Wolf looked at Horseman. And then he smiled.

"I won't tell," Horseman said. His voice was loud, rising almost to a scream. And then he turned and ran, ran frantically down the dry wash which drained away from the prairie-dog colony. And behind him he heard the Wolf laughing.

2

That night the Wind People moved across the Reservation. On the Navajo calendar it was eight days from the end of the Season When the Thunder Sleeps, the 25th of May, a night of a late sliver of moon. The wind pushed out of a high-pressure system centered over the Nevada plateau and carved shapes in the winter snowpack on San Francisco peaks, the Sacred Mountain of Blue Flint Woman. Below, at Flagstaff airport, it registered gusts up to thirty-two knots—the dry, chilled wind of high-country spring.

On the west slope of the Lukachukai Mountains, the Wind People whined past the boulder where Luis Horseman was huddled, his body darkened by ashes

to blind the ghosts. Horseman was calm now. He had
thought and he had made his decision. The witch had
not followed him. The man in the dog skin didn't
know him, had no reason to destroy him. And there
was no place else to hide. Soon Billy Nez would know
he was on this plateau and would bring him food,
and then it would be better. Here the Blue Policeman
could never find him. Here he must stay despite the
Navajo Wolf.

Horseman opened his medicine pouch and inspected the contents. Enough pollen but only a small
pinch of the gall medicine, which was the best proof
against the Navajo Wolves. He removed the turquoise
bear and set it on his knee.

"Horn of the bica, protect me," he chanted. "From
the Darkness to Be One, protect me." He wished, as
he wished many times now that he was older, that he
had listened when his uncle had taught him how to
talk to the Holy People.

A hundred miles south at Window Rock, the Wind
People rattled at the windows of the Law and Order Building, where Joe Leaphorn was working his
way through a week's stack of unfinished case files.
The file folder bearing the name of Luis Horseman
was third from the bottom and it was almost ten
o'clock when Leaphorn reached it. He read through
it, leaned back in his chair, lit the last cigarette in his

pack, tapped his finger against the edge of his desk and thought. *I know where Horseman is. I'm sure I know. But there is no hurry about it. Horseman will keep.* And then he listened to the voices in the wind, and thought of witches, and of Bergen McKee, his friend who studied them. He smiled, remembering, but the smile faded. Bergen, himself, was the victim of a witch—the woman who had married him, and damaged him, and left him to heal if he could. And apparently he couldn't.

He considered the letter he had received that week from McKee—talking of coming back to the Reservation to continue his witchcraft research. There had been such letters before, but McKee hadn't come. And he won't come this time, Leaphorn thought. Each year he waits to pick up his old life it will be harder for him. And maybe now it's already too hard. And, thinking that, Leaphorn snapped off his desk lamp and sat a moment in the dark listening to the wind.

At Albuquerque, four hundred miles to the east, the wind showed itself briefly in the apartment of Bergen McKee, as it shook the television transmission tower atop Sandia Crest and sent a brief flicker across the face of the TV screen he wasn't watching. He had turned off the sound an hour ago, intending to grade final-examination papers. But the wind made him nervous. He had mixed a shaker of martinis instead, and drank slowly, making them last until, finally, he could sleep.

Tomorrow, perhaps, there would be the answer to his letter, and Joe Leaphorn would tell him that it was a good season for witchcraft gossip, or a poor season, or a fair season. And maybe, if prospects were good, he would go to the Reservation next week and spend the summer completing the case studies he needed to finish the book that no longer mattered to him. Or maybe he wouldn't go.

He snapped on the radio and stood by the glass door opening on his apartment balcony. The wind had raveled away the cloud cover over Sandia Mountain and its dark outline bulked against the stars on the eastern horizon.

Ten stories below, the lights of the city spread toward the foothills, a lake of phosphorescence in an infinity of night. Behind him the radio announced that tomorrow would be cooler with diminishing winds. It then produced a guitar and a young man singing of trouble.

"But," the singer promised, "life goes on.

"And years roll by,
And time heals all,
And soon we're dead,
We're peaceful dead."

The sentiment parodied McKee's mood so perfectly that he laughed. He walked back to his desk—a bulky, big-boned, tired-faced man who looked at once powerful and clumsy. He shuffled the ungraded exam papers together, dumped them into his briefcase, poured a final martini from the shaker, and took it into the bedroom. He looked at the certificate framed on the wall. It needed dusting. McKee brushed the glass with his handkerchief.

"Whereas," the proclamation began, "it is commonly and universally known by all students of Anthropology that Bergen Leroy McKee, B.A., M.A., Ph.D., is in truth and in fact none other than MONSTER SLAYER, otherwise identified as the Hero Twin in the Navajo Origin Myth;

"And Whereas this fact is attested and demonstrated by unhealthy obsession and preoccupation of said Professor McKee, hereafter known as MONSTER SLAYER, with belaboring his students with aforesaid Origin Myth;

"And Whereas MONSTER SLAYER is known to have been born of Changing Woman and sired by the Sun;

"And Whereas the aforesaid sexual union was without benefit of Holy Matrimony, and is commonly known to have been illicit, illegal, unsanctified and otherwise improper fornication;

"Therefore be it known to all men that the afore-said MONSTER SLAYER meets the popular and legal definition of Bastard, and demonstrates his claim to this title each semester by the manner in which he grades the papers of his Graduate Seminar in Primitive Superstition."

The proclamation had been laboriously hand-lettered in Gothic script, embossed with a notary public's seal, and signed by all seven members of McKee's seminar. Signed six years ago, the year he had won tenure on the University of New Mexico anthropology faculty—full membership in the elite of the students of man with W. W. Hill, and Hibben, Ellis and Gonzales, Schwerin, Canfield, Campbell, Bock and Stan Newman, Spuhler, and the others. The year he became part of a team unmatched between Harvard and Berkeley. The last good year. The year before coming home to this apartment and finding Sara's closets empty and Sara's note. Fourteen words in blue ink on blue paper. The last year of excitement, and enthusiasm, and plans for research which would tie all Navajo superstitions into a tidy, orderly bundle. The last year before reality.

McKee drained the martini, switched off the lights and lay in the darkness, hearing the wind and remembering how it had been to be Monster Slayer.

3

Bergen McKee approached his faculty mailbox on the morning of May 26 as he habitually approached it—with a faint tickle of expectation. Years of experience, of pulling out notices to the faculty, lecture handbills, and book advertisements, had submerged this quirk without totally extinguishing it. Sometimes when he had other things on his mind, McKee reached into the box without this brief flash of optimism, the thought that today it might offer some unimaginable surprise. But today as he walked through the doorway into the department secretary's outer office, said good morning to Mrs. Kreutzer, and made the right turn to reach the mail slots, he had no such distraction. If the delivery was as barren as usual, he would be required to turn his thoughts immediately to the problem of grading eighty-four final-examination papers by noon tomorrow. It was a dreary prospect.

"Did Dr. Canfield find you?" Mrs. Kreutzer was holding her head down slightly, looking at him through the top half of her bifocals.

"No ma'am. I haven't seen Jeremy for two or three days."

The top envelope was from *Ethnology Abstracts*. The form inside notified him that his subscription had expired.

"He wanted you to talk to a woman," Mrs. Kreutzer said. "I think you just missed her."

"O.K.," McKee said. "What about?" The second envelope contained a mimeographed form from Dr. Green officially reminding all faculty members of what they already knew—that final semester grades must be registered by noon, May 27.

"Something about the Navajo Reservation," Mrs. Kreutzer said. "She's trying to locate someone working out there. Dr. Canfield thought you might know where she could look."

McKee grinned. It was more likely that Mrs. Kreutzer had decided the woman was unattached and of marriageable age, and might—in some mysterious way—find McKee attractive. Mrs. Kreutzer worried about people. He remembered then that he had met a woman leaving as he came into the Anthropology Building, a young woman with dark hair and dark eyes.

"Was she my type?" he asked. The third and last letter was postmarked Window Rock, Arizona, with the return address of the Division of Law and Order, Navajo Tribal Council. It would be from Joe Leaphorn. McKee put it into his pocket.

Mrs. Kreutzer was looking at him reproachfully, knowing what he was thinking, and not liking his tone. McKee felt a twinge of remorse.

"She seemed nice," Mrs. Kreutzer said. "I'd think you'd want to help her."

"I'll do what I can," he said.

"Jeremy told me you were going to the reservation with him this summer," Mrs. Kreutzer said. "I think that's nice."

"It's not definite," McKee said. "I may have to take a summer-session course."

"Let somebody else teach this summer," Mrs. Kreutzer said. She looked at him over her glasses. "You're getting pale."

McKee knew he was not getting pale. His face, at the moment, was peeling from sunburn. But he also knew that Mrs. Kreutzer was speaking allegorically. He had once heard her give a Nigerian graduate student the same warning, and when the student had asked him what Mrs. Kreutzer could possibly have meant by it, McKee had explained that it meant she was worrying about him.

"You ought to tell them to go to hell," Mrs. Kreutzer said, and the vehemence surprised McKee as much as the language. "Everybody imposes on you."

"Not really," McKee said. "Anyway, I don't mind."

But as he walked down the hall toward his office he did mind, at least a little. George Everett had asked him to take his classes this summer, because Everett had an offer to handle an excavation in Guatemala, and it irritated McKee now to remember how sure Everett had been that good old Bergen would do him the favor. And he minded a little being the continuing object of Mrs. Kreutzer's pity. The cuckold needs no reminder of his horns and the reject no reminder of his failure.

He took the Law and Order envelope from his pocket and looked at it, neglecting his habitual glance through the hallway window at the chipping plaster on the rear of the Alumni Chapel. Instead he thought of how it had been to be twenty-seven years old in search of truth on the Navajo Reservation, still excited and innocent, still optimistic, not yet taught that he was less than a man. He couldn't quite recapture the feeling.

It wasn't until he had opened the blinds, turned on the air conditioner and registered the familiar creak of his swivel chair as he lowered his weight into it that he opened the letter.

Dear Berg:

I asked around some in re your inquiry about witchcraft cases and it looks only moderately promising. There's been some gossip down around the No Agua Wash country, and an incident or two over in the Lukachukais east of Chinle, and some talk of trouble west of the Colorado River gorge up on the Utah border. None of it sounds very threatening or unusual—if that's what you're looking for. I gather the No Agua business involves trouble between two outfits in the Salt Cedar Clan over some grazing land. The business up in Utah seems to center on an old Singer with a bad reputation, and our people in the Chinle subagency tell me that they don't know what's going on yet in the Lukachukai area. The story they get (about fourth-hand) is that there's a cave of Navajo Wolves somewhere back in that west slope canyon country. The witches are supposed to be coming around the summer hogans up there, abusing the animals and the usual. And, as usual, the stories vary depending on which rumor you hear.

The first two look like they fit the theories
expressed in Social and Psychotherapeutic
Utility of Navajo Wolf and Frenzy Superstitions, *but you should know, since you wrote it.*
I'm not sure about the Lukachukai business. It
might have something to do with a man we're
looking for up there. Or maybe it's a real genuine
Witch, who really turns himself into a werewolf
and wouldn't that knock hell out of you scientific
types?

There were two more paragraphs, one reporting
on Leaphorn's wife and family and a mutual friend
of their undergraduate days at Arizona State, and the
other offering help if McKee decided to "go witch-
hunting this summer."

McKee smiled. Leaphorn had been of immense
help in his original research, arranging to open the
Law and Order Division files to him and helping him
find the sort of people he had to see, the unaccultur-
ized Indians who knew about witchcraft. He had
always regretted that Leaphorn wouldn't completely
buy his thesis—that the Wolf superstition was a simple scapegoat procedure, giving a primitive people
a necessary outlet for blame in times of trouble and
frustration.

He leaned back in the chair, rereading the letter
and recalling their arguments—Leaphorn insisting

that there was a basis of truth in the Navajo Origin Myth, that some people did deliberately turn antisocial, away from the golden mean of nature, deliberately choose the unnatural, and therefore, in Navajo belief, the evil way. McKee remembered with pleasure those long evenings in Leaphorn's home, Leaphorn lapsing into Navajo in his vehemence and Emma—a bride then—laughing at both of them and bringing them beer. It would be good to see them both again, but the letter didn't sound promising. He needed a dozen case studies for the new book—enough to demonstrate all facets of his theory.

Jeremy Canfield walked in without knocking. "I've got a question for you," he said. "Where do you look on the Navajo Reservation for an electrical engineer testing his gadgets?"

He extracted a pipe from his coat pocket and began cleaning debris from the bowl into McKee's ashtray. "Just one more helpful hint. We know he has a light-green van truck. We don't know what kind of equipment it is, but this research needs to be away from such things as electrical transmission lines, telephone wires, and stuff like that."

"That helps a lot," McKee said. "That still leaves about ninety percent of the Reservation—ninety percent of twenty-five thousand square miles. Find one green truck in a landscape bigger than all New England."

"It's this daughter of a friend of mine. Girl named Ellen Leon," Canfield said. "She's trying to find this bird from U.C.L.A." He was a very small man, bent slightly by a spinal deformity, with a round, cheerful face made rounder by utter baldness.

"Goddamn flatlanders never know geography," Canfield said. "Think the Reservation's about the size of Central Park."

"Why's she looking for him?" McKee asked.

Canfield looked pained.

"You don't ask a woman something like that, Berg. Just imagine it's something romantic. Imagine she's hot for his body." Canfield lit the pipe. "Imagine she has spurned him, he has gone away to mend a broken heart, and now she has repented."

Or, McKee thought, imagine she's a fool like me. Imagine she's been left and is still too young to know it's hopeless.

"Anyway, I told her maybe in the Chuska Range, or the Lukachukais if he liked the mountains, or the Kam Bimghi Valley if he liked the desert, or up there north of the Hopi Villages, or a couple of other places. I marked a map for her and showed her where the trading posts were where he'd be likely to buy his supplies."

"Maybe they're married," McKee said. He was interested, which surprised him.

"Her name's Ellen Leon," Canfield said with emphatic patience. "His is Jimmy W. Hall, Ph.D. Besides, no wedding ring. From which I deduce they're not married."

"O.K., Sherlock," McKee said. "I deduce from your attitude that this woman was about five feet five, slim, with long blackish hair and wearing . . ." McKee paused for thought, ". . . a sort of funny-colored suit."

"I deduce from that that you saw her in the hall," Canfield said. "Anyway, I told her we'd keep our eyes open for this bird and let her know where we'd be camping so she could check." He looked at McKee. "Where do you want to start hunting your witches?"

McKee started to mention Leaphorn's letter and say he hadn't decided yet whether to go. Instead he thought of the girl at the front entrance of the Anthropology Building, who had looked tired and disappointed and somehow very sad.

"I don't know," McKee said. "Maybe down around No Agua, or way over west of the Colorado gorge, or on the west slope of the Lukies." He thought a moment. Canfield's current project involved poking into the burial sites of the Anasazis, the pre-Navajo cliff dwellers. There were no known sites around No Agua and only a few in the Colorado River country. "How about starting over in those west slope canyons in the Lukachukais?"

"That's good for me," Canfield said. "If you've got some witches in there to scrutinize, there's plenty of ruins to keep me busy. And I'll take my guitar and try to teach you how to sing harmony."

At the door, Canfield paused, his face suddenly serious.

"I'm glad you decided to go, Bergen. I think you need . . ." He stopped, catching himself on the verge of invading a zone of private grief. "I think maybe I should ask a guarantee that your witches won't get me." It came out a little lamely, not hiding the embarrassment.

"My Navajo Wolves, being strictly psychotherapeutic, are certified harmless," McKee said. He pulled open a desk drawer, rummaged through an assortment of paper clips, carved bones, arrow heads and potsherds, and extracted an egg-sized turquoise stone, formed roughly in the shape of a crouching frog. He tossed it to Canfield.

"Reed Clan totem," McKee said. "One of the Holy People. Good for fending off corpse powder. No self-respecting Navajo Wolf will bother you. I guarantee it."

"I'll keep it with me always," Canfield said.

The words would come back to McKee later, come back to haunt him.

4

Bergen McKee had spent most of the afternoon in the canvas chair beside the front door in Shoemaker's. It was a slow day for trading and only a few of The People had come in. But McKee had collected witchcraft rumors from three of them, and had managed to extract the names of two Navajos who might know more about it. It was, he felt, a good beginning.

He glanced at Leaphorn. Joe was leaning against the counter, listening patiently to another of the endless stories of Old Man Shoemaker, and McKee felt guilty. Leaphorn had insisted that he needed to go to the trading post—that he had, in fact, delayed the call to take McKee along—but more likely it was a convenient piece of makework to do a friend a graceful favor.

"There is a young man back in there we want to pick up," Leaphorn had said. He pushed a file folder across the desk. "He cut a Mexican in Gallup last month."

The file concerned someone named Luis Horseman, aged twenty-two, son of Annie Horseman of the Red Forehead Clan. Married to Elsie Tso, daughter of Lilly Tso of the Many Goats Clan. Residence, Sabito Wash, twenty-seven miles south of Klagetoh. The file included three arrest reports, for drunk and disorderly, assault and battery, and driving while under the influence of narcotics. The last entry was an account of the knifing in a Gallup bar and of a car stolen and abandoned after the knifing.

"What makes you think he's over in the Lukachukai country?" McKee had asked. "Why not back around Klagetoh with his wife?"

"It isn't very complicated," Leaphorn had said. Horseman probably thought he had killed the Mexican and was scared. His in-laws detested him. Horseman would know that and know they would turn him in, so he had run for the country of his mother's clan, where he could stay hidden.

"How the devil can you find him, then?" McKee had asked. "It would take the Marine Corps to search those canyons."

And Leaphorn had explained again—that the

knife victim was now off the critical list and that if the good news was gotten to Horseman one of two things would happen. He would either turn himself in to face an assault charge, or, being less frightened, would get careless and show up in Chinle, or at Shoemaker's, or some other trading post. Either way, he'd be picked up and the file closed.

"And so I go to Shoemaker's today and spread the word to whatever Red Foreheads come in, and one of them will be a cousin, or a nephew, or something, and the news gets to Horseman. And if you don't want a free ride you can stay and help Emma with the housework."

And now Leaphorn was spreading the word again, talking to the big bareheaded Navajo who had been collecting canned goods off the shelves. "He's sort of skinny," Leaphorn was saying, "about twenty-two years old and wears his hair the old way."

"I don't know him," the Big Navajo said. He inspected Leaphorn carefully, then moved to the racks where the clothing was hung. He tried on a black felt hat. It was several sizes too small, but he left it sitting ludicrously atop his head as he sorted through the stock.

"My head got big since the last time I bought a hat," the Navajo said. He spoke in English, glancing at McKee to see if the white man appreciated Navajo clowning. "Have to have a seven-and-a-half now."

"Get that hair cut off and you could wear your old hat," Shoemaker said.

The Big Navajo wore braids, in the conservative fashion, but very short braids. Maybe, McKee thought, he had had a white man's haircut and was letting it grow out.

"Some son of a bitch stole the old one," the Big Navajo said. He tried on another hat.

McKee yawned and looked out the open door of the trading post. Heat waves were rising from the bare earth in front. To the northeast a thunderhead was building up in the sky over Carrizo Mountain. It was early in the season for that. Tomorrow was Wednesday. McKee decided he would accept Leaphorn's invitation to spend another day with him. And then he would take his own pickup and try to find the summer hogan of Old Lady Gray Rocks. He would start with her, since she was supposed to be the source of one of the better rumors. And by Thursday when Canfield arrived they would move into Many Ruins Canyon, set up camp, and work out of the canyon.

The Big Navajo had found a hat that fitted him, another black one with a broad brim and a high crown—the high fashion of old-generation Navajos. He looked like a Tuba City Navajo, McKee decided, long-faced and raw-boned with heavy eyebrows and a wide mouth.

"O.K.," the man said. "How much do I owe you now?"

The Big Navajo had taken a silver concho band from his hip pocket. He let it hang over his wrist while he handed Shoemaker the bills and waited for his change. The metal glowed softly—hammered discs bigger than silver dollars. McKee guessed the conchos would bring $200 in pawn. He looked at the big man with new interest. The Navajo was slipping the silver band down over the crown of his hat.

"This Horseman," Leaphorn was saying, "cut up a Mexican over in Gallup. Got drunk and did it, but the Nakai didn't die. He's getting better now. They want to talk to Horseman about it over at Window Rock."

"I don't know anything about him," the big man said.

"He's the son of Annie Horseman," Leaphorn said. "Used to live back over there across the Kam Bimghi, over on the west slope of the Lukachukais." He indicated the direction, Navajo fashion, with a twitch of his lips.

The Big Navajo had been picking up his box of groceries. He put it down and looked at Leaphorn a moment and then ran his tongue over his teeth, thoughtfully.

"Whereabouts on the west slope?" he asked. "Law and Order know where he is?"

"General idea," Leaphorn said. "But it would be better if he came on in himself. You know. Otherwise we'll go in there and get him. Make it worse for everybody."

"Horseman," the Big Navajo said. "Is he . . ."

Leaphorn was waiting for the rest of the question.

"What'd you say this kid looks like?"

"Slender fellow. Had on denims and a red shirt. Wears his hair the old way and ties it back in a red sweatband."

"I don't know him," the big man said. "But it would be good if he came in." He hoisted the box under his arm and walked toward the door.

"This man's a college professor," Leaphorn said, pointing to McKee. "He's looking for some information out here about witches."

The Navajo shook hands. He looked amused.

"They say there's a Wolf over toward the Lukachukais," McKee said. "Maybe it's just gossip."

"I heard some of that talk." He looked at McKee and smiled. "It's old-woman talk. A man out there's supposed to had a dream about the Gum-Tooth Woman and about a three-legged dog coming into his hogan and he woke up and he saw this dog in his brush arbor, and when he yelled at it, it turned into a man and threw corpse powder on him."

The Navajo laughed and slapped McKee on the shoulder.

"Horse manure," he said. "Maybe the Wolf is this boy the policeman is hunting for." He looked at Leaphorn. "I guess you'll be after that boy if he don't come in. Are you hunting for him now?"

"I don't think we're looking very hard yet," Leaphorn said. "I think he'll come in to see us."

The Big Navajo went through the door.

"Be better if he came in," he said.

It was almost sundown when Leaphorn pulled the Law and Order carryall onto the pavement of Navajo Route 8 at Round Rock. Two hours' drive back to Window Rock.

"Pretty fair day's work for me," McKee said. "But I think you wasted your time."

"No. I got done about what I wanted."

McKee was surprised.

"You still think Horseman's back in there? Nobody had seen him."

Leaphorn smiled. "Nobody admitted they'd seen him. There wasn't any reason for them to admit it. They know how the system works. But that old man who came in the wagon . . ." Leaphorn picked his clipboard of notes off the dashboard and inspected it. "Nagani Lum, it was. He damned sure knew something about it. Did you notice how interested he was?"

"Lum was one who was telling me about a witching case," McKee recalled. "Pretty standard stuff." A two-headed colt had been born. Lum hadn't seen it but a relative had. The brother-in-law of an uncle, as McKee remembered it. And then the boy who herded sheep for his uncle's brother-in-law had actually seen the Navajo Wolf. Thought it was a dog bothering the sheep, but when he shot at it with his .22, he saw it had turned into a man. But it was getting dark and he didn't think he'd hit it. As usual, McKee thought, it was a little too dark to really see and, as usual, the source was a boy.

"I think that joker who was buying himself the new hat knew something about Horseman, too," Leaphorn was saying. "The one who was kidding you about your witch stories."

"He said he didn't."

"He also said somebody stole his hat."

"What do you mean?" McKee asked.

"Did you see that concho hatband? Why would anybody steal an old felt hat and leave behind all that fancy silver?"

They had passed Chinle now, Leaphorn driving the white carryall at a steady seventy. The highway skirted the immense, lifeless depression which falls away into the Biz-E-Ahi and Nazlini washes. It was lit now by the sunset, a fantastic jumble of eroded geological formations. The white man sees the desolation and calls it a desert, McKee thought, but the Navajo name for it means "Beautiful Valley."

"Can you tell me why that man would lie about somebody stealing his hat?" Leaphorn asked. His face was intent with the puzzle. "Or, if he wasn't lying, who would steal an old felt hat and leave that silver band behind?"

5

Joseph Begay awakened earlier than usual. He lay still a moment, allowing consciousness to seep through him, noticing first the predawn chill and that his wife had captured most of the blankets they shared. Then he registered the rain smells, dampened dust, wet sage, piñon resin and buffalo grass. Now fully awake, he remembered the sudden midnight shower which had awakened them in the brush arbor and driven the family to shelter in the hogan. Through the open hogan door, he saw the eastern horizon was not yet brightening behind the familiar upthrusting shape of Mount Taylor, seventy miles away in New Mexico. Reaches for the Sky was one of the four sacred mountains which marked the four corners of the Land of the People, and Joseph Begay thought, as he had thought many mornings, that he had chosen this site well. The old hogan which he and his brothers-in-law had built near his mother-in-law's place had been located on low ground, near water but closed in with the hills. He had never liked the site. When the son they had called Long Fingers had died of the choking sickness in the night—died so suddenly that they had not had time to move him out of the hogan so that the ghost could go free—he had not been sorry that they had to leave the site. He had boarded up the door himself and covered the smoke hole so the ghost of Long Fingers would not bother his in-law people and had decided right away that this place on the mesa would be the place for the new hogan.

And, when he had built it, he had not faced the door exactly east as the Old People had said it must be faced, but very slightly north of east so that when he awoke in the morning he would see Reaches for the Sky outlined by the dawn, and remember that it was a place of beauty where Changing Woman had borne the Hero Twins. It would be a good thought to awaken with, and because he had not made the door exactly east he had been very careful to follow the Navajo Way with the remainder of the construction. He had driven a peg and used a rope to mark off the circle to assure that the hogan wall would be round and of the prescribed circumference. He had put the smoke hole in exactly the proper place and, when he had plastered the stones with adobe, he had sprinkled a pinch of corn pollen on the mud and sung the song from the Blessing Way.

Joseph Begay slipped off the pallet and pulled on his pants and shirt, moving silently in the darkness to avoid awakening his wife and two sons, who slept across the hogan. He moved around their feet, with the Navajo's unconscious care not to step over another human being, and ducked through the door. His boots, forgotten in the brush arbor, were only slightly damp. He put them on as he heated water for a cup of coffee.

He was a short, round-faced man with the barrel chest characteristic of a Navajo-Pueblo blood mixture, from a clan which had captured Pueblo brides and with them the heavier, shorter bone structure of the Keresan Indians. He poured the coffee into a mug and sipped it while he ate a strip of dried mutton. The rain had been light, a brief shower, but it was a good omen.

He knew the Callers of the Clouds had been at work on the Hopi and Zuñi reservations and that along the Rio Grande, far to the east, the Pueblo Indians were holding their rain dances. The magic of these pueblo dwellers had always been strong, older than the medicine of the Navajos and more potent. It was a little early for this first shower and Begay knew that was promising.

Begay finished his coffee before he allowed his thoughts to turn to his reasons for rising early. In a very few hours he would see his daughter, his daughter whom he hadn't seen since last summer. He would drive to the bus stop at Ganado, and the bus would come and he would put her suitcases and her boxes in the pickup truck and drive with her back to the hogan. She would be with them all summer. Begay had deliberately postponed thinking about this, because the Navajo Way was the Middle Way, which avoided all excesses—even of happiness. The shower at midnight and the smell of the earth and the beauty of the morning had been enough. But now Begay thought of it as he started the pickup truck and drove in second gear down the bumpy track across the mesa. And, as he drove, he sang a song his great uncle had taught him:

> "I usually walk where the rains fall.
> Below the east I walk.
> I being Born of Water,
> I usually walk where the rains fall.
> Within the dawn I walk.

I usually walk where the rains fall.
Among the white corn I walk.
Among the soft goods I walk.
Among the collected waters I walk.
Among the pollen I walk.
I usually walk where the rain falls."

It was brightening on the eastern horizon as he shifted into low gear to wind down the switchback, descending the long slope toward the highway. It took almost fifteen minutes, and at the bottom, skirting the base of the mesa, was Teastah Wash. If it had rained harder elsewhere on the mesa, he might not be able to drive through the wash until the runoff water cleared. He stopped just as his truck tilted down the steep incline, put on the emergency brake, and stepped out. The headlights, illuminating the bottom of the wash, showed only a slight trickle of water across the sandy expanse. What little runoff there had been was mostly gone now.

It was when he was turning to climb back into the pickup that he saw the owl. It flew almost directly at the truck, startling him, flitted through the headlight beams, and disappeared abruptly in the dawn half-light up the wash. He sat behind the wheel a moment, feeling shaken. The owl had acted strangely, he thought, and it was known that ghosts sometimes took on that form when they moved in the darkness. It looked like a burrowing owl, Begay thought, but maybe it was a ghost returning with the dawn to a grave or a death hogan.

He was still thinking of the owl as he let the pickup ease slowly down the steep bank and then raced it across the soft bottom. And he was thinking of it as the truck climbed out of the arroyo, its motor laboring in low gear. But by now the mood of the morning had recaptured him and he thought that it was just a burrowing owl, going home from the night's hunting and confused by his headlights. It was just beyond the rim of the shallow canyon, just after the pickup had regained level ground and he had shifted into second gear, that he saw that he was wrong.

The body lay just beside the track and his headlights first reflected from the soles of its shoes. Before he could stop, the pickup was almost beside it. Joseph Begay shifted into neutral and left the motor running. He unbuttoned his shirt and extracted a small leather pouch hung from his neck by a thong. The pouch contained a small bit of jet flint in the crude shape of a bear, and about an ounce of yellow pollen. Begay put his thumb in the pollen and rubbed it against his chest. He chanted:

"Everywhere I go, myself
May I have luck,

Everywhere my close relatives go
May they have their good luck."

The ghost was gone—at least for the moment. He had seen it flying up Teastah Wash. He got out of the truck and stood beside the body. It was a young man dressed in jeans and a red shirt and with town shoes on. The body lay on its back, the legs slightly parted, right arm outflung and left arm across the chest with the wrist and hand extending, oddly rigid. There was no visible blood but the clothing was damp from the rain.

As Begay drove the last mile down the bumpy track toward the highway, driving faster than he should have, he thought that he would have to report this body to Law and Order before he went to the bus station. He tried not to think of the expression frozen on the face of the young man, the dead eyes bulging and the lips drawn back in naked terror.

6

It was **midmorning** when the news of Horseman reached Leaphorn's office. In the two hours since breakfast, McKee had sorted through two filing cabinets, extracted Manila folders marked "Witchcraft" and segregated those identified as "Wolf" from those labeled "Frenzy" and "Datura." The datura cases involved narcotics users, and most frenzy incidents, McKee knew, centered on mental illness. If he had time, he'd look through those later. He was marking Wolf incident locations on a Bureau of Indian Affairs reservation map, coding them with numbers, and then making notes of names of witnesses, when the radio dispatcher stopped at the door and told Leaphorn that Luis Horseman had been found.

"When did he come in?"

"Found his body," the dispatcher said.

Leaphorn stared at the dispatcher, waiting for more.

"The captain wants to know if you can pick up the coroner and clear the body?"

"Why don't they handle it out of the Chinle sub-agency?" Leaphorn asked. "They're a hundred miles closer."

"They found him down near Ganado. You're supposed to pick up the coroner there."

"Ganado?" Leaphorn looked incredulous. "What killed him? Suicide?"

"Apparently natural," the dispatcher said. "Too much booze. But nobody's looked at him yet."

"Ganado," Leaphorn said. "How the devil did he get down there?"

It was forty-five minutes to Ganado and Leaphorn spent most of them worrying to McKee about being wrong.

"Congratulations," McKee said. "You're forty years old and you just made your first mistake."

"It's not that. It just doesn't make sense." And then, for the third time, Leaphorn reviewed his reasoning—looking for a flaw. The Gallup police had reported the car Horseman had taken after the knifing was last seen heading north on U.S. 666, the right direction. It had been found later, abandoned near Greasewood. The right place, if he was returning to the west-slope canyon country of his mother's clan. And there was every reason to think he would. Horseman was scared. The territory was empty, and a fugitive's dream for hiding out. His kinsmen would feed him and keep their mouths shut. And at Shoemaker's Leaphorn was certain that at least two of those he had talked to had known about Horseman. There was the old man with the witch story and it was even more obvious with the boy who had come in late. He had clearly been relieved to hear the Mexican hadn't died and clearly was in a hurry to end the conversation and go tell someone about it. And then there was the Big Navajo. "He was interested," Leaphorn said. "Remember he asked me to describe Horseman. And Shoemaker said he was new around there. Why would he be interested if he hadn't seen him?"

"You're hung up on the hat thing," McKee said.

"All right," Leaphorn said. "You explain the hat."

"Sure. He took the hatband off and while it was off, somebody stole the hat."

"When's the last time you took off your hatband?"

"I don't wear silver conchos on my hat," McKee said.

They picked up the coroner-justice of the peace at

a Conoco station in Ganado, a man named Rudolph Bitsi. Bitsi told them to drive south.

The late morning sun was hot by the time they arrived at the edge of Teastah Wash and the Navajo policeman who had been left with the body had retreated into the shade of the arroyo wall. He climbed into the sunlight, blinking, as the carryall stopped. He looked very young, and a little nervous. Leaphorn said the policeman was Dick Roanhorse, just out of recruit school.

"Find anything interesting?" Leaphorn asked.

"No, sir. Just this bottle. The only tracks are the ones made by Begay's pickup. Rain washed everything else out."

"The body was here before the rain, then," Leaphorn said. It was more a statement than a question, and the policeman only nodded.

Leaphorn pulled the blanket off the body. They looked at what had been Luis Horseman.

"Well," Bitsi said, "looks like he might have had some sort of seizure."

"Looks like it," Leaphorn said.

Bitsi squatted, examining the face. He was a short, middle-aged man, tending to fat, and he grunted as he lowered himself. He sniffed at Horseman's nose and lips.

"Alcohol. You can just barely get a whiff of it."

Leaphorn was looking at Horseman's legs. McKee noticed they were rigidly straight—as if he had died erect and tumbled backward, which wasn't likely.

Bitsi was still examining the face. "I saw one that looked like that two, three years ago. Crazy bastard had made him a brew out of jimson weed to get more potent and it poisoned him."

Leaphorn was looking at Horseman's left arm. The watch on his wrist was running, which would mean he had wound it the previous day—probably less than twenty-four hours earlier. It was a cheap watch, the kind that cost about $8 or $10, with a stainless-steel expansion band. Leaphorn stared at the left hand. The arm lay across Horseman's chest with the wrist and hand extended, unsupported.

"Pretty fair booze," Bitsi said, holding up the bottle. The label was red and proclaimed the contents to be sour-mash whiskey. About a half ounce of amber liquid remained in the bottle.

"Looks like he overdid it," Bitsi said. "Looks like he strangled. Fell down while he was throwing up, and passed out and strangled."

"That's what it looks like," Leaphorn said.

"Might as well haul him in," Bitsi said. He rose from his squat, grunting again.

"No tracks at all?" Leaphorn asked the policeman.

"Just Begay's. Where he got out of his pickup and came over to look at the body. Nothing but that."

There were plenty of tracks now. Mostly Roanhorse's, Leaphorn guessed.

"Where was the bottle?"

"Four or five feet from the body," Roanhorse said. "Like he dropped it."

"O.K.," Leaphorn said. He was looking across the flat through which Teastah Wash had eroded, an expanse of scrubby creosote bush with a scattering of sage. At the lip of the wash bank, a few yards upstream from the road, two small junipers had managed to get roots deep enough to live. Leaphorn walked suddenly to the nearest bush and examined it. He motioned to Roanhorse, and McKee followed.

"You pull a limb off this for anything?"

Roanhorse shook his head.

There was a raw wound on the lower trunk where a limb had been broken away. Leaphorn put his thumb against the exposed cambium layer and showed it to McKee. It was sticky with fresh sap.

"What do you think of that?"

"Nothing," McKee said. "How about you?"

"I don't know. Probably nothing."

He started walking back toward the body, through the creosote bush, searching. Bitsi, McKee noticed, had climbed back into the carryall.

"Look around across the road there," Leaphorn said, "and see if you can find that juniper branch."

But he found it himself. The frail needles were dirty and broken. McKee guessed it had been used as a broom even before Leaphorn told him.

"That looked pretty smart, Joe," McKee said. "Where does it take you?"

"I don't know." Leaphorn was looking intently at the body. "Notice how his legs are stretched out straight. He could have pushed 'em out that way after he fell down, but if you do that laying on the ground, looks like it would push your pants cuffs away from your ankles." He stood silently, surveying the body. "Maybe that's all right though. It could happen." He looked at McKee. "That wrist couldn't happen, though."

He squatted beside the body, looking up.

"Ever try to pick up an unconscious man? He's limp. Absolutely limp. After he's dead two-three hours, he starts getting stiff."

That's why I noticed the arm, McKee thought. It doesn't look natural.

"You think he was dead, and somebody put him here?"

"Maybe," Leaphorn said. "And whoever did it didn't know it was going to rain so they brushed out their tracks."

"But why?" McKee asked. He looked around. Here the body was sure to be found and down in the wash it could have been buried, probably forever.

"I've got better questions than that," Leaphorn said. "Like how did he die? We can find that out. And then maybe it will be who did it, and why. Why would anyone want to kill the poor bastard?"

7

Old Woman Gray Rocks leaned back against the cedar pole supporting one corner of the brush hogan and took a long pull on the cigarette McKee had lit for her. She blew the smoke out her nostrils. Behind her, the foothills of the Lukachukais shimmered under the blinding sun—gray mesquite and creosote bush, gray-green scrub cedar, and the paler gray of the eroded gullies, and above the grayness the blue-green of the higher slopes shaded now by an embryo early-afternoon thundercloud. By sundown, McKee thought, the cloud would be producing lightning and those frail curtains of rain which would, in arid-country fashion, evaporate high above the ground. He wondered idly if Leaphorn had been right—if

Horseman had been hiding back in that broken canyon country.

He refocused his eyes to the dimmer light under the brush and saw that Old Woman Gray Rocks was smiling at him.

"The way they do it," she said, "is catch the Wolf and tie him down. Not give him anything to eat or any water and not let him take his pants down for anything until he tells that he's the one that's doing the witching. Once they tell it, it's all right after that. Then the witching turns around and the man he did it to gets all right and the witch gets sick and dies."

Old Woman Gray Rocks removed the cigarette and held it between thumb and first finger. It occurred to McKee that every Navajo he had ever seen smoking—including children—used the same unorthodox grip.

"I don't think they're going to catch this one," she said.

"Why do you say that?" McKee was feeling good that his command of Navajo had returned. Two days ago he would only have said "Why?" which required a single monosyllabic guttural. He had only had time for one afternoon in the language lab listening to tapes and his pronunciation had been rough at first. Now he was almost as fluent as he had been at twenty-seven. "Kintahgoo' bil i noolhtah?" he said, repeating the question and relishing the sound.

"They don't think he lives around here. He's a stranger."

McKee was suddenly mildly interested. He had been feeling drowsy, the effect of an unusually heavy meal (lamb stew, floating in fat, boiled corn, fried cornbread, and canned peaches) and of a certainty, established not long after Canfield had dropped him off at the hogan, that the woman would tell him nothing useful. He had hoped he would learn something of the motivation behind the witchcraft gossip, detect the sickness, or the intra-family tensions, or the jealousies, or whatever trouble had produced a need for a scapegoat witch. This hope had grown when Old Woman Gray Rocks had proved friendly and welcomed him warmly. All morning long it had faded. But there was nothing to do now but wait for Canfield to stop on his way back from buying supplies to pick him up. If there was serious trouble in the clan, natural or human, Old Woman Gray Rocks seemed genuinely unaware of it. She gossiped cheerfully about minor affairs. The nephew of an uncle by marriage had left his wife and taken up with a woman in the Peach Tree Clan at Moenkopi. He had stolen one of his wife's horses. One of the sons of Hosteen Tom had gone to Farmington to join the Marine Corps but they said now that he was working at the place where they mined the coal near Four Corners. They said the Marines didn't take him because he didn't do right on the papers.

There had been much other information. The winter had been wet and early grazing was pretty good. The price of wool was down a little but the price of mutton was up. Some of the nephews had found jobs at the new sawmill the Tribal Council had opened. George Charley had seen trucks way over by Los Gigantes Buttes and the men told him they belonged to an oil company and that Hosteen Charley had better move his sheep out of there because they would be shooting off dynamite. Old Woman Gray Rocks thought this was strange and McKee had not felt his Navajo good enough to undertake an explanation of how seismograph crews record shock waves in searching for petroleum deposits.

Until now, only two of her remarks had been worth remembering. She had mentioned that a man driving a truck had stopped her sister's husband and asked him about a road. McKee had asked her about that, thinking of Miss Leon's misplaced electrical engineer. The road had been the one which leads into Many Ruins Canyon. Old Woman Gray Rocks said the driver had been a Belacani like McKee and the truck had been pulling a little two-wheel trailer, and it was like those they haul bread in, with a door in the back—which meant it might be a van, like Dr. Hall's van. She didn't know what color it was but her grandson had seen it parked in Hard Goods Canyon three or four weeks ago when he was trapping rabbits. Hard Goods was the wash that runs into Many Ruins Canyon about nine miles up from the mouth, she said.

And then Old Woman Gray Rocks had returned to the subject of the decline of the younger generation, and mentioned a cousin of her nephews had cut up a Nakai in Gallup and stolen a car and run away.

"I heard about that at Window Rock," McKee said. "I heard his name was Luis Horseman." He checked an impulse to tell her that Horseman was dead and to ask her if the cousin of her nephews had come home to hide. It was better to let her talk.

"That's his name," Old Woman Gray Rocks said. She spit on the ground. "He always acted like he didn't have any relatives. Got drunk all the time and fought people. His mother wasn't any good either. Run off from her children." She lit another cigarette.

McKee wondered how far Leaphorn's news had spread. "Did he kill that man in Gallup?"

"They say he got well," she said. "A policeman came to Shoemaker's and said that, and said he should come in to talk to Law and Order. It would be better if he did that."

"How's he going to know?"

Old Woman Gray Rocks looked toward the Lukachukais. "They said somebody went back in there
and told him about it," she said. "I think it was one of
those boys in the Nez outfit went to tell him."

And that, McKee thought, will tell Joe Leaphorn
that he guessed right about Horseman coming home
to hide. And maybe it will tell him somebody named
Nez saw Horseman the evening before his body
turned up. That gave him a chance to return one of
Leaphorn's many favors.

And now it seemed that this gossipy woman
knew more about the witching incidents than she
had been willing to admit. He thought about her
statement that the Wolf was a stranger. A few hours
earlier he would have rejected such an idea as incon-
gruous. The witch should be one of the clan, a known
irritant or target of envy. But now he was faced with
a new set of facts. There seemed to be, if Old Woman
Gray Rocks was well informed, none of the usual
causes to produce a scapegoat witch. The cause, when
he found it, now would likely be something isolated
and outside the usual social pattern. He decided to
pursue this point very gingerly.

"Who is the Navajo who says this Wolf is a
stranger?" McKee asked.

"I heard that from my husband. He said they told

him that one of the Tsosie boys found the place in an arroyo over that way"—Old Woman Gray Rocks made a vague gesture with her lips toward the Luka-chukai slopes—"where the Wolf had camped. It was a dry camp and there was a spring just a mile up the arroyo. If he lived around here he would have known where the water was."

"How did they know it was the Wolf's camp?" McKee asked.

"They said to my husband that the boot tracks were the same tracks that Tsosie Begay found around his sheep pen after the Wolf came there."

So, thought McKee.

"Is this boy of the family of Charley Tsosie?" he asked.

"It is the son of Charley," Old Woman Gray Rocks said. "He didn't get married so he is still with the clan."

"And the Tsosie place is the one the Wolf came to?"

"That's what is said. Charley Tsosie was one of them he bothered."

"Do you know the name of the other ones?" McKee asked. Before their meal she had assured him that she didn't know the identity of anyone who claimed to be troubled by a Wolf. McKee considered this small lie, now gracefully retracted, not as an indication of a

Navajo secrecy but as a further demonstration of the mystery of womanhood. He had no theory concerning why Old Woman Gray Rocks had withheld this information earlier, and no theory concerning why she had decided to confide it to him now, and no idea whether she would tell him more. McKee had concluded years ago that the intricacies of feminine logic were beyond his comprehension.

Old Woman Gray Rocks seemed not to have heard the question. She was looking down the slope toward the pole corral, where two young grandsons were putting a saddle on a scrubby-looking horse.

"I heard at the trading post that the other one the Wolf came after was a man they called Afraid of His Horse," McKee said. "But someone else said that wasn't right. And someone else told it was a fellow named Shelton Nakai, but they didn't know where he lived now."

"Who told you it was Afraid of His Horse?" Old Woman Gray Rocks asked.

"I don't remember who it was now," McKee said. It had been Mr. Shoemaker at the trading post, and Shoemaker had also told him that Afraid of His Horse was the son-in-law of Old Woman Gray Rocks.

"Maybe it was Ben Yazzie the witch was after," the woman said slowly. "I don't know where he lives now. He used to graze some sheep way up on the high slopes over there by Horse Fell and Many Ruins Canyons. That's where he used to have his summer hogan."

McKee thought she looked nervous, and he thought he knew why. She didn't want her son-in-law connected, even in gossip, with witching, so she was turning his attention to Yazzie. He would find Charley Tsosie, Ben Yazzie, and Afraid of His Horse later, and talk to them, but now he would change the subject. He wanted to learn more, if Old Woman Gray Rocks would tell him, about why this witch was thought to be a stranger.

"I don't know why they think this Wolf doesn't live around here," McKee said. "Maybe he made that dry camp in the arroyo because he thought somebody would come to the spring and he didn't want them to find him."

"Somebody saw him one night," the old woman said. She spoke very slowly, weighing what she would say, and how much she would say. "Witches come out mostly when there is a moon and there was a moon that night. This man he woke up in the night and heard a coyote singing and he went out to see about some lambs he had penned up out there and he saw the witch there in the moonlight. It wasn't anyone who has his hogan around here."

McKee started to ask the name of this man, and

thought better of it. This "someone" would be Afraid of His Horse, the old woman's son-in-law.

"But how did this man know he was seeing a witch?" McKee asked. "Maybe it was just somebody walking through there."

McKee thought, for a long moment, that Old Woman Gray Rocks would ignore the question. He let it hang in the heavy silence. Behind the winter hogan, the dogs began to bark and McKee heard the sound of the pickup truck—Canfield coming back from Shoemaker's with the groceries.

"The way I heard it," Old Woman Gray Rocks said, still slowly, "this witch had a wolf skin over his back and he was down where those rams were penned, killing them with a knife."

Canfield arrived from Shoemaker's with $43 worth of groceries in the camper, a case of beer, and a letter from Ellen Leon, postmarked Page, Arizona. She planned to spend a day or two checking the trading posts around Mormon Ridge and the Kaibab Plateau in the northwest section of the Reservation. And then she would come to Chinle on Thursday and drive over to Shoemaker's trading post and find out where she could meet them. Canfield had left a note and a penciled map telling her they would be camped about five miles up the main branch of Many Ruins Canyon and showing her how to get there.

"Works out good for everybody," Canfield said. "You've got your witchery business going on in the neighborhood, and if we have time, we can look around up in there and see if we can find that green van." He grinned. "Let's hope we don't find it. We'll get out my guitar and serenade her and spend bacchanal evenings under the Navajo moon."

"I don't know if I've got any witchery business yet," McKee said. "I've got to find this Tsosie family and find out what their trouble is, if anything. According to the old lady, Charley usually has his summer hogan just a few miles south of where we'll be camping, so that should be easy. Then maybe the Tsosies can tell me where to find Afraid of His Horse. The old lady didn't want to talk about him. They don't like witch trouble in the family."

"What are you going to do about Horseman?"

McKee thought about it. "I think I ought to go on back to Chinle tomorrow and call Leaphorn about it," he said.

"Your cop really think it wasn't a natural death?"

"I don't think he knows," McKee said. "But he guessed right about Horseman coming back in here to hide."

Canfield let the pickup idle along the hard-packed sand of the canyon floor, turning occasionally to side canyons to check his map and his memory of where cliff ruins he would inspect were located. The sun was low as they penetrated the upper canyon. Here the cliffs closed in, rising in sheer, almost smooth walls nearly four hundred feet to a narrow slit of sky above. Here in this slot of eroded stone darkness came early. Canfield had switched on his headlights before he found a likely camp—a hillock of rocky debris which had collected enough soil to support an expanse of grass and even a growth of young cottonwoods and willows.

By the time they had Canfield's working tent pitched and supper cooked, the first stars were visible over the canyon walls. A nighthawk flashed past them, hunting. Up canyon a rasping hoot touched off a dull pattern of echoes.

"Saw-whet owl," Canfield said. He grinned at McKee. "If Leaphorn was right, maybe that's Horseman's ghost enjoying the night out."

They ate and then sat in the silent darkness, watching the light of the early moon light the top of the canyon walls. From some infinite distance came the faint sound of barking.

"Take your pick," McKee said. "A coyote, some sheepherder's lost dog, or one of my witches turned into a wolf for the evening."

Canfield took the turquoise frog from his pocket and rubbed it, chuckling.

"I'll say it's a witch," he said, "because this keeps me safe from witches."

Actually, McKee remembered, the turquoise shape wasn't a Navajo charm. It was a much older Anasazi fertility totem with nothing at all to do with witches.

Of course it didn't really matter.

8

McKee left the campsite before dawn, called Leaphorn's office from the Gulf station on the highway at Chinle, and then ate a leisurely breakfast at Bishbito's Diner while he waited for the policeman to make the sixty-mile drive from Window Rock. Leaphorn arrived while he was finishing his third cup of coffee. He handed McKee a sheet of paper and sat down.

"Take a look at that," he said. "And then let's go and find that boy who went to warn Horseman."

The paper was a carbon of an autopsy report form:

SUBJECT: Luis Horseman (war name unknown).
AGE: 23.
ADDRESS: 27 miles southwest of Klagetoh.

NEXT OF KIN: Wife, Elsie (Tso) Horseman,
Many Goats Clan.

TIME OF DEATH: Between 6 P.M. and 12 midnight, June 11 (estimated).

CAUSE OF DEATH: Suffocation. Substantial accumulation of fine granular material in lung
tissue, windpipe, throat and nostrils.

There was more information, negative reports on
blood alcohol and on abrasions and concussions, and
an analysis indicating the "fine granular material"
was common silica-based sand.

"The medical examiner said it looked like he got
caught in a cave-in," Leaphorn said. "Like he had
been buried in sand."

"You think so?"

"And somebody dug him out? And laid him out
there at Teastah Wash with the bottle of whiskey he
hadn't drunk?" Leaphorn thought about his own
questions. "I don't know. Maybe. But there wasn't
any sand in his cuffs, or in his pockets, or anywhere
else."

"It wouldn't make any sense anyway," McKee
said.

Leaphorn was looking out the window. "I think
I know a lot about witches," he said. "You think you
know a lot about witches. How do you kill a witch?"

The question surprised McKee. He thought about it. "You mean do you smother them?"

"Remember that case over at Fruitland?" Leaphorn asked. "That guy whose daughter died of t.b.? He shot four of them. And then there was that old Singer up near Teec Nos Pas a couple of years ago. He was beaten to death."

"There's no special way that I know of," McKee said. "There was supposed to be a hanging back in the 1930's but there wasn't any proof and they think it was just gossip. Usually, though, it's heat-of-passion stuff—beating, shooting, or knifing. Something like that. Why? You think somebody thought Horseman was a witch?"

"Makes a certain amount of sense," Leaphorn said. "But I don't know." He was still staring out the window. "Why kill somebody like Horseman? Just another poor soul who didn't quite know how to be a Navajo and couldn't learn to act like a white. No good for anything."

McKee could think of nothing to say. Out the window there was the highway, the asphalt strip of Navajo Route 9, and across it to the east, the blue-gray mass of the Lukachukai Range. He wondered what Leaphorn was seeing out there.

"I was in charge of the Shiprock subagency when that Fruitland thing happened," Leaphorn said.

"That one was mine. I heard that Navajo Wolf talk and I didn't pay much attention to it and so we had five bodies to bury."

"Four," McKee said.

"No. It was five." Leaphorn turned, smiling grimly. "This isn't Salem," he said. "We don't recognize witchcraft legally and the guy shot an old Hand Trembler and his wife, and a schoolteacher and her husband, and then he shot himself. Didn't want to stand trial for murder."

"What are you trying to do?" McKee asked. "Figure out a way to blame yourself for Horseman?"

"I could have gone in and looked for him."

"But not found him," McKee said. "Besides, Horseman wasn't a stranger. The old woman said the Wolf is a stranger."

"Yeah," Leaphorn said. "That's what she said. Maybe she had a reason to lie. Let's go find that boy who went out to warn Horseman." He looked at his notes. "Billy Nez. Let's go find Billy and see what he knows."

But finding Billy Nez was not possible.

They found his family's hogans east of Chinle, not far from Shoemaker's, but not Billy. His uncle was sore about it.

"Kid took a horse and took off after breakfast," he said. "He's gone all the time. Screwing around back up in the mountains somewhere, when he's supposed to be helping out."

Would he be back tonight? The uncle couldn't guess. Sometimes he was gone for days. He and Leaphorn talked a moment and then the lieutenant returned to the carryall, and turned it back toward Chinle.

"Found out a little," Leaphorn said. "The boy knew where Horseman was hiding—somewhere back up in those canyons. But when he went to tell him he hadn't killed anybody, Horseman was gone." Leaphorn paused. "Or at least the kid said he was gone."

"You don't think he was?"

"Probably," Leaphorn said. "The uncle also told me something else. Billy Nez is Horseman's younger brother."

"His brother?" McKee said. "How about the different name?"

"Family broke up," Leaphorn said. "Billy was living with his uncle so he used Nez instead of Horseman. You know how it is with the Dinee. The only name that really counts is the war name you get when you're little. And that one's a secret inside your family and it's only used in your Blessing Way ceremonial or if you get somebody to sing you a cure."

It was noon when they reached the Chinle sub-agency office and the man Leaphorn wanted to see was at lunch. They found him at the diner, and Leaphorn introduced him as Sam George Takes. He was a round-faced, barrel-chested young man, wearing the uniform of a Law and Order sergeant. McKee ordered chicken-fried steak, more lunch than he usually allowed himself.

"Hell, you know how it is, Joe," Takes was saying. "It's summer, school's out. He's probably chasing some girl and no telling when he gets back."

"That's right," Leaphorn said. "That's what you do when you're sixteen or so. Hanging around some girl's hogan. Or, if your brother is missing, maybe looking for your brother."

Takes put down his fork. "And he don't find him and he comes home and his uncle sends him in here like he said he would and we find out whatever he knows, which is probably nothing, and that's the end of it. Why are you worrying?"

"It could work out like that," Leaphorn said. "But you know how news travels on this reservation. It could be by now he knows his brother is dead. So maybe he connects it to this witching gossip. Then he collects some cousins and uncles and goes looking for the Wolf."

McKee's lunch arrived, with the gravy poured over the French fries.

"Al's cook quit again," Takes said. "Son of a bitch is trying to do his own cooking."

"The problem is where to start looking," Leaphorn said. "It's your territory, Sam. Where do you think?"

Takes looked glum. "Son of a bitch could be anywhere. You remember when we had that bootlegger in there working a still right after the Korean War. We never did find him." Takes looked as though the thought still irritated him. "We knew he had to be close to water and at least have a horse to haul the grain in, but booze came out of there for four years and we never found nothing."

"It wouldn't take that Nez outfit four years to find itself a witch," Leaphorn said.

Takes laughed. "If you're worrying about that," he said, "they're going to have an Enemy Way. That ought to take care of the witch."

"Who's having it?" Leaphorn asked. "Somebody in the Nez family?"

"I heard it was Charley Tsosie," Takes said. "But they're Nez kinfolks—part of the same outfit."

McKee was interested. Old Lady Gray Rocks had mentioned Tsosie being bothered by the witch. But the Prostitution Way was the curing ceremonial held for those exposed to witchcraft—to turn the evil around and direct it back against the Wolf who started it. Why an Enemy Way? McKee thought about the rite. It had grown out of the fighting between the Dinee and the Utes, and the only times he

had heard of its being used was when members of
The People came home after being off the Reservation, people like discharged servicemen, people who
had been in contact with foreign influences—white
men, or Pueblo Indians, or Mexicans. He remembered again what the old woman had said about the
witch being a stranger. Leaphorn was looking at him.

"If they're having an Enemy Way, that old
woman must have told you right," Leaphorn said.
"They think it's an outsider, and if they think that,
they didn't think it was Horseman and that wasn't
why he was killed."

"Wonder why he was," Takes said. "Usually
there's a feud, or fighting over a woman, or somebody
bad-mouthing somebody."

"Maybe he found that whiskey still you were
looking for," McKee said.

"Hasn't been any bootleg whiskey turning up in
years," Takes said.

"How about that rocket the military lost
three, four years ago?" Leaphorn said. "Is that ten-
thousand-dollar reward still out for anyone finding
that thing?"

"I don't know," Takes said. "I don't think they
ever found it."

"I'll call the people up at the Tonepah Range and
find out if they're still offering ten thousand dollars,"

Leaphorn said. He explained to McKee that missiles fired from the Tonepah test site in Utah to the impact area at White Sands Proving Grounds in New Mexico passed over the empty eastern expanse of the Reservation.

"They used to lose one now and then when a second stage misfired, and then they'd have a hell of a time finding it," Leaphorn said. "But now they have a radar station over on Tall Poles Butte and they track 'em all the way to the ground."

"You think maybe Horseman and somebody else both found the old rocket and fought over who'd get the reward?" McKee asked.

Leaphorn shrugged. He asked Bishbito if he could use his office telephone for a long-distance call.

McKee finished his meal, eating dutifully, feeling simultaneously disappointed and ashamed of that disappointment. He had once again, as he had for years, fallen victim to his optimism. Expecting something when there was always nothing. Anticipating some romantic mystery in what Takes and Leaphorn must already see as a sordid, routine little homicide. It was this flaw, he knew, that had cost him these last eight years of anguish, turned to misery, turned to what now was simply numbness. He could still see the note, blue ink on blue paper in Sara's easy script:

"Berg. I am meeting Scotty in Las Vegas tonight. I won't contest the divorce."

Simply that, and her signature. It was not Sara's style to add the unnecessary explanation, to say that he was a dull, nondescript man in a dull, dead-end job, and that Scotty was exciting, in an exciting world of money and executive jets and Caribbean weekends. He cursed himself as he always did when he thought of it, cursed the flaw that made him ignore the fact that he was a clumsy, unbrilliant, average man, grotesquely misfit in the circle of slim, cool Saras and reckless, witty Scotts.

He turned away from the memory and thought of Horseman, another failure as a man, wondering why he had let himself expect anything exotic in his death. And then he turned away from that thought, too. Horseman was none of his business. He would get back to his research, now. The Charley Tsosie family would be busy, taking ritual sweat baths and preparing for their curing ceremonial. But there was still Ben Yazzie to be interviewed and Afraid of His Horse to be found.

He flipped through his notebook. Old Lady Gray Rocks had said Ben Yazzie grazed his sheep back on the Lukachukai plateau in the summer. He would go to the subagency office and find out where Yazzie and Afraid of His Horse had their hogans. And then he would get on with his interviewing. He reread the notes he had accumulated at Shoemaker's and from talking to the old woman. Nothing much on Afraid of His Horse, but the Yazzie gossip followed the usual pattern. A man at the trading post had said Yazzie had noticed a coyote following him, and since the coyote was the messenger of the Holy People, Yazzie had accepted this as a sign of danger. And then there had been the usual sounds in the night, interpreted as the witch trying to put corpse powder down the smoke hole in the hogan roof, and the usual dead lambs, and the usual third-hand account in which Yazzie had seen a dog hanging around the flock and, when the dog ran away, it turned into a man.

Leaphorn was returning from his telephone call; McKee returned the notebook to his pocket. He would start with Yazzie this afternoon.

"Well," Leaphorn said, "there went our motive." He sat down. "The colonel said the reward expired two years ago. Their lost bird is obsolete now." He laughed. "In fact, I think he's hoping it stays lost. Sort of embarrassing to lose one like that and then have it turn up after everybody's forgotten about it."

"So we're right back noplace," Takes said.

"I had an idea," McKee said. "Let's say somebody else was hiding out back in that area and they didn't

want the Navajo police coming in with a search party.
Let's say they decided the way to keep that from happening was to get Horseman out where he would be
found."

As he said it, McKee realized it sounded hope-
lessly farfetched, but Leaphorn's face was grim.

"I thought of that, too," he said. "The autopsy
showed he was killed between six and midnight the
day I was at Shoemaker's telling everybody we were
going in after him if he didn't come out. If we figure
it that way, I'm the one who got him killed."

9

Bergen McKee honked the horn of his pickup when he crossed the final eroded ridge and saw the hogan of Ben Yazzie on the slope below. It was an unnecessary gesture—since the engine could have been heard long before the horn—but a courteous one. It gave official notice to the hogan that a visitor was coming and McKee guessed it was a universal custom among rural people. His father, he remembered, would never approach another's farmhouse without pausing at the gate to holler, "Hello," until properly acknowledged. Among people who depended more upon distance from neighbors than window blinds to preserve their privacy it was a practical habit.

The place consisted of two octagonal hogans of unpeeled ponderosa logs, a small plank storage shack, and two brush arbors, all built in a cluster of cedar at the edge of a small arroyo. Just over the lip of the arroyo, two sheep pens had been built of cedar poles, with the arroyo bank furnishing one wall. The pens were empty now, and as McKee coasted his truck slowly past them he saw that the hogans were equally deserted.

No cooking pots hung under the brush shelter, no clothing hung out to air, none of the accumulated odds and ends of Navajo living cluttered the area. He climbed out of the truck and sat in the scanty shade, feeling tired and disappointed.

McKee lit a cigarette and considered his next step. In time, he could relocate the Yazzie family through Shoemaker. They traded there and some of Ben Yazzie's silver concho belts were in pawn there. But it might be weeks before any of the Yazzie family, or anyone who knew where he had moved, showed up at the store. That left just two possible sources in the Many Ruins area: Afraid of His Horse, whose sheep camp was supposed to be somewhere north of the canyon, and Charley Tsosie. Tsosie would be occupied at the Enemy Way for at least two days. Sheep camp tended to move with the grazing and would be hard to find. But he would look for Afraid of His Horse.

It was easy to see why Yazzie had built his hogan here. Behind the habitations, the sandstone cliffs of a butte rose abruptly to the north and west—a hundred centuries of talus at its base, then two hundred feet of sheer, smooth reddish stone, with streaks of dark discoloration from seepage, then a softer gray layer of perlite, pocked and carved with blowholes and caves, and above this the overhanging cap of hard, black igneous rock. It gave the hogans shelter from the southwest winds and shade from the late-afternoon sun. To the north and east, the country was a fantastic jumble of colossal erosion dominated by another towering flat-topped butte. All the colors of the spectrum are there, McKee thought. Everything but pure green. What little grass there was out of sight, hidden in the pockets where soil could collect to hold roots and where runoff from the immensity of rocks could be held and absorbed. He had passed several such grassy places following the wagon trail here. Some, he had noticed, had been heavily grazed by sheep. Most had not. Yazzie must have been badly frightened to move his flock away from grass.

The clouds were building now above the Lukachukai peaks and McKee thought there might be a thunder shower over Many Ruins Canyon by sundown. He and Canfield had camped well up off the floor of the canyon, safe from flash floods, but he had left most of his gear outside the tent. Canfield might be there to take care of things, or he might be out digging into the burial site at one of the ruins; when he was working, Canfield could not be depended upon to notice it was raining.

McKee butted out his cigarette and pushed himself to his feet, noticing the stiffness of his muscles and thinking ruefully that sitting behind a desk was poor conditioning for a field trip. It was then he noticed the smell.

It was a faint smell, borne on a sudden light breeze which had fanned up the arroyo past the hogans. McKee recognized it instantly. The smell of death and decaying flesh. He stood stock-still beside the truck, studying the silent hogans. If the odor had come from them, he would have noticed it earlier. He walked slowly down the slope. Beyond the brush arbor he stopped and stood silently again, listening. Behind the hogans, the arroyo curved sharply around a high outcropping of rock topped by a growth of juniper and piñon. Something behind this ridge was making a sound, a tuneless symphony of low notes which would not have been audible except for the otherwise eerie silence of the place. He walked slowly toward the trees, listening, feeling the tenseness of irrational nervousness. Then the sound explained itself.

A raven flapped out of one of the piñons with a raucous caw. A second later a cloud of the black scavenger birds erupted from the arroyo in an explosion of flapping. McKee stood a moment feeling simultaneously weak from the sudden start and foolish at his skittishness. He trotted to the top of the ridge to see what had attracted the scavengers.

In the arroyo bend, against the perpendicular wall of eroded sandstone, Ben Yazzie had built a third pole sheep corral. In it were bodies of five rams with the heavy dark wool of Merinos. Looking directly down into the pen, McKee could see its floor was blackened in several places where blood had soaked into the sand. He could also see that the ravens, now raising a noisy clamor from the trees fifty yards down the arroyo, had been at work on the throats of the animals. That meant, McKee thought, they had been killed by a wolf, or coyotes, or perhaps by dogs.

It took almost exactly an hour for McKee to cover the nine miles of wagon road from the Yazzie hogans to the mouth of Many Ruins Canyon. Even before he left the place he had concluded that the dead rams, and the cause of their death, probably explained the origin of at least some of the witchcraft gossip. When he found Yazzie he would learn that Yazzie had lost many sheep to this "witch" and that he had decided to abandon his traditional grazing grounds and his hogan because a witch is, after all, more than a man can be expected to cope with. Yazzie would not be likely to admit, even to himself, that he could not deal with coyotes, or even with an unusually bold wolf of the natural, four-legged variety. When McKee found Afraid of His Horse, he would learn the coyotes were also active this season north of Many Ruins. Taken together, he thought, the two linked incidents would provide the first of the specific examples he needed to support his scapegoat thesis. He felt suddenly optimistic.

It was not until he had turned the truck up the sandy bottom of Many Ruins Canyon that McKee realized that he wasn't sure exactly how a coyote could have gotten into the rams' pen. The pen was built in a rough half-circle extending from the arroyo wall. McKee remembered he had not been able to look over the pen from the arroyo bed. That meant the pole wall was about six feet high—too high for a coyote, or even a wolf, to jump. It occurred to him then that Yazzie must surely have built the corral with coyotes or wolves much in mind and designed it to keep them out. The poles were wired together, top and bottom, and the bases had been buried in the sandy soil. The gate, a narrow door of poles held together by horizontal braces, had also been wired securely shut. McKee remembered this clearly because of the time it had taken him to unfasten the wires. If Yazzie had carelessly left the gate insecurely fastened the night the wolf got in, why would he have bothered to fasten it so securely after the damage was done?

McKee drove slowly along the hard-packed canyon floor. The cloud he had noticed earlier had built higher now and there had been a shower somewhere. The breeze was cool and smelled of wet pine. In places the going was slow and rocky. Here the canyon walls closed in, sheer smooth cliffs which funneled the water of the occasional flash floods into a narrow torrent. But generally the road was smooth and the canyon bottom broadened to a hundred yards or more. The runoff stream here required only a small portion of the canyon floor. Its bed wandered between tumbled hills of rocky debris and there were grass and even a few cottonwoods. Here the sandstone had been softer and more readily destroyed by wind and water. It was in places like these that the Anasazis had built on the talus slopes and high under the overhanging shelter of the canyon walls the cliff houses which gave the canyon its name. McKee passed three of these stone ruins on his way to the campsite without giving them more than a glance. He was, by then, thoroughly disgusted with himself for his oversight at the sheep pens—carelessness which meant he would have to return to the Yazzie hogans and find out exactly how the coyotes had gotten in. He was so immersed in this problem that it was not until he turned his truck up the slope to the campsite that he noticed Canfield's camper truck was gone.

McKee switched off the ignition and sat silently a

moment. The exhaust noise echoed up and down the canyon and then died, leaving an utter stillness. The butane campstove was unlit, McKee noticed, and there was no sign that Canfield had started cooking supper, although it was his turn for the chore.

"Where in the devil could he have gone?" McKee said aloud. He was inside the tent when he saw the note, a sheet of typing paper on the folding table weighted by a turquoise frog—Canfield's proof against witches.

> *Bergen—*
> *A Navajo dragged himself up here with a leg all swollen up with snakebite. I'm taking him to Teec Nos Pas. Be back tomorrow morning.*
>   *JOHN*

McKee reread the note and stared at the signature; Dr. J. R. Canfield's first name was Jeremy, not John.

10

Sandoval squatted beside the sand painting and told Charley Tsosie to put his knees on the knees of the Corn Beetle. He showed him how to lean forward with one hand on each hand of the figure. When Tsosie was just right, Sandoval began singing the part about how the corn beetles called out to tell the Changing Woman that her Hero Twins, the Monster Slayer and the Water Child, were coming home again safely. His voice rose in pitch on the "lo-lo-loo" cry of the beetle, and then fell as he chanted the part about the Hero Twins visiting the sun, and slaughtering the monster Ye-i. It was stifling in the hogan and Tsosie's bare back was glistening with sweat. Even his loin cloth was discolored with it. That was good. The enemy was coming out. And now Sandoval was ready for the next part. He sprinkled a pinch of corn pollen on Tsosie's shoulders and had him stand up and step off the sand painting—carefully so that the pattern wouldn't be disturbed.

Sandoval felt good about the painting. He hadn't done an Enemy Way since just after the foreign war when the young men had come back from the Marines. He was afraid he might have forgotten how to do it. But it had worked out just right. The arroyo sand he had poured out on the hogan floor for the base was a little darker than he liked but he had known it was going to work all right when he poured out the colored sand to make the Encircling Guardian. He had made it in a square as his father had taught him, with the east side open to keep from trapping in any of the Holy People. The Guardian's head was at the north end, with his two arms inward, and his feet were at the south end. His body was four alternating lines of red and yellow sand, and at the opening Sandoval had drawn the elaborate figure of Thunder, wearing the three crooked arrows in his headdress and carrying the crooked arrows under his wings.

"Put Thunder there when you sing for a witching," his father had told him. "His lightning kills the witches."

Sandoval repaired the Corn Beetle deftly, sifting colored sand through his fingers to reform the lines where Tsosie's hands and knees had pressed. He added a tiny sprinkle of black sand to the single feather in the headdress of Big Fly.

Sandoval stood up then and looked into the pot where he had brewed the medicine. The water was still steaming and the juniper leaves he had mixed into it had turned the solution milky. It looked about right but Sandoval thought it would have been better if he had had a waterproof basket so it could have been done the old way. The People are losing too many of the old ways, Sandoval thought, and he thought it again when he had to tell Tsosie how to sit on the feet of Big Fly, and even had to remind him to face the east. When Sandoval was a boy learning the ways from his father, his father had not had to tell people how to sit. They knew.

Sandoval sang then the chant of the Big Fly, and how he had come to The People to tell them that Black God and the warriors were returning victorious from their war against the Taos Pueblo and how the two girls had been sent by the people to carry food to the war band. This was the last chant before the vomiting and Sandoval was glad of that. It was the second day of the Enemy Way. His voice was hoarse and he was tired and there was still much to be done, much ritual to be completed before this man was free of the witch trouble. His daughter had been right and he should have listened to her. He was eighty-one (or eighty-two by the white man's way of counting) and loaded with too many years to conduct a three-day Sing like an Enemy Way.

Sandoval dipped the ceremonial gourd into the pot, filling it with the hot, milky fluid, and handed the gourd to Tsosie.

"Drink all of it," he ordered, thinking you shouldn't have to tell a man that. And, while Tsosie drank, he sang the last two chants. He refilled the gourd and handed it to Agnes Tsosie and then to the two sons. Let the others get their own, Sandoval thought, and he ducked past the double curtains hung over the hogan doorway to see if the time was right.

Outside the air was cool, almost cold after the closeness of the hogan. The eastern horizon was turning from red to yellow and Sandoval saw it was about the right time. He pulled back the curtains and called to Tsosie.

"Go out there behind the brush shelter," he ordered, "and remember that to make it right you want to vomit out the witching just as you can see the top rim of the sun coming up." When Tsosie came past the curtain, Sandoval handed him a chicken feather.

"Just when the sun is first coming up," Sandoval

reminded him. "If the medicine isn't working, stick that feather down your throat."

Sandoval sat on the ground and leaned back on the wall of the hogan, relishing the coolness. He would have about thirty minutes before the vomiting was finished and then one more chant to sing while Tsosie and his family were rubbing the juniper stew on their bodies. Then it would be time for the people from the Stick Receivers to arrive. Sandoval yawned and stretched and looked out across the brush flats where the visitors were camping. Probably four or five hundred, he thought, and there would be more arriving today, mostly women bringing their girls to look for husbands at the Girl Dance tonight, and young men looking for girls, and gambling, and drinking, and trouble. Sandoval had meant to think about the ceremonial, to think just good thoughts and keep in harmony with the event. But he couldn't help thinking how times were changing. Mostly they came in their pickups and cars now. There were dozens of them parked out there and just a few wagons. And that was part of it. The white man's machines made it easy to travel about and people came just to visit and fool around. In the old days there wouldn't have been any drinking and gambling at a ceremonial like this. Sandoval watched a white carryall with the humped buffalo insignia of Law and Order drive up across the flat, and a man in blue jeans and a checked shirt get out of it and talk to a woman starting a cook fire near one of the pickups. The woman pointed in Sandoval's direction and the man came walking toward him.

He was short, with heavy shoulders and a Roman nose, and when he stopped in front of Sandoval and said, "My grandfather, I hope all is well with you," his voice was very clear and distinct. Sandoval, who had noticed lately that most young people mumbled, liked this. He invited the young man to sit beside him.

"I am called Joe Leaphorn," the young man said, "and I work for Law and Order," but after that he talked about other things—about the rains starting early this year, which was good, and about drinking and gambling at the ceremonials, which was bad. Sandoval approved of this, knowing that the policeman would get around to his business in good time and appreciating that here was a young one who knew the old and patient ways.

"There has not been an Enemy Way in this country in a long time," the policeman said, and from the way he said it, Sandoval thought that the time had come for business.

"I guess," the policeman added, "that they had a Star Gazer, or a Hand Trembler come." It was not a question, exactly, but the tone confirmed Sandoval's guess. The policeman was talking business now.

"Hand Trembler," Sandoval said. "They got Jimmy Hudson to come out here and hold his hand over Charley Tsosie and Hudson found out he had been witched. Hudson said the witch blew something on him."

"There was a man lived out here who they called Luis Horseman," the policeman said. "I wonder if he was a witch?"

"I don't know about him."

"I guess the Enemy Way will work even if you don't know who the witch is. But, my grandfather, I am an ignorant man about many things. There were no Singers in my family and I don't know how the Scalp Shooter gets the scalp if you don't know who the witch is."

"They know something about him," Sandoval said. He was enjoying this. Enjoying the young man's finesse and the sparring with words.

"I knew a Hand Trembler once who was wrong. He said a ghost had got at my uncle's brother's son and they had a Shooting Way Sing for that. Turned out he had tuberculosis."

"Hand trembling's not much good usually," Sandoval agreed. "But this time he got it right. They said this Navajo Wolf came down and bothered Tsosie's sheep in the night and Tsosie saw him. Looked like a big coyote but it was a man. And then after Hudson came and hand trembled, they got one of the outfit who knew some of the chants and they did a blackening on Tsosie and after that he felt better for a little while." Sandoval hadn't liked the remark about tuberculosis. He wondered sourly if the young man believed in witches. The policeman had a white man's haircut. Not the way the Changing Woman had taught. He was looking out across the sagebrush flat now, thinking. Sandoval guessed the next question would tell him something.

"My grandfather, I am using too much of your time today, but I keep wondering about this. I know you have never listened to gossip but I will tell you something you might need to know for your Sing. This man Horseman is dead now, and if he was the witch, you might need to know about it for the way you hold the Sing."

Sandoval wondered why the policeman thought a man named Horseman was the witch. The question would come now. Maybe it would tell him.

"As I said, I am ignorant about many things. I know it would be easier to cure Tsosie if the witch was already dead. But how would be the best way to kill the witch?"

Sandoval turned the question over carefully. "The best way is with clubs."

The policeman was looking at him closely now.

"Would it be a good thing to smother him? To pour sand over his head?"

"I never heard that. Sometimes with clubs and sometimes they shoot them." Sandoval was puzzled. He had never heard of Horseman and he had never heard of a man being killed like that. He saw Tsosie was coming back now from behind the brush shelter and he got to his feet. His bones felt stiff and he was irritated. He suspected the young man had left the Navajo Way and was on the Jesus Road.

"My grandson, I must go back into the hogan now. But now I have a question for you to answer. Tell me if you believe in witching."

"My father taught me about it," the policeman said. "When the water rose in the Fourth World and the Holy People emerged through the hollow reed, First Man and First Woman came up, too. But they forgot witchcraft and so they sent Diving Heron back for it. They told him to bring out 'the way to get rich' so the Holy People wouldn't know what he was getting. And Heron brought it out and gave it to First Man and First Woman and they gave some of it to Snake. But Snake couldn't swallow it so he had to hold it in his mouth. And that's why it kills you when a snake strikes you."

The words were right, Sandoval thought, but he recited them like a lesson.

"You didn't tell me whether you believe it."

The man named Leaphorn smiled very slightly.

"My grandfather," he said, "I have learned to believe in evil."

Lieutenant Joe Leaphorn had returned to his carryall intending to get some sleep. He had left Window Rock a little after midnight to drive to the Tsosie place. But the track over the slick rock country had been even worse than he remembered and the two hours' rest he had hoped to have when he arrived had been used in low-gear driving over the great waste of eroded slopes west of the Lukachukais. Now he had time. He had learned nothing positive from Sandoval. He had asked around and learned that Billy Nez was not yet here. There was nothing to do but wait. The sun, now rising, would have to be halfway up the sky before it was time for the Encounter Between the Camps and then there would be the exchange of gifts and other ritual before the scalp shooting could be held. He leaned back against the seat, feeling exhausted but wide awake. He found himself again retracing all he knew of Luis Horseman, again examining each assorted fact for some semblance of pattern.

The file on Luis Horseman at Window Rock had been typical of those for the relatively few young men who gave Law and Order the bulk of its business. A few scattered years of schooling on the Reservation, arrests at Gallup and Farmington and Tuba City for drunk and disorderly, beginning when he was seventeen. Short-term jobs on the Santa Fe railroad maintenance crews and at the strip mine. A marriage into the Minnie Tso family, a fight, a six-month term in the tribal jail for aggravated assault, and then the knifing at Gallup and the stolen car. All that was familiar enough. Too familiar.

"He acted like he had no relatives," Leaphorn thought and grinned wryly at the old-fashioned expression. When he was a boy, it was the worst thing his mother could say about anyone. But then the Navajo Way made the relatives totally responsible for anything one of the family did. Now that was changing and there were more young men like Horseman. Souls lost somewhere between the values of The People and the values of the whites. No good even at crime.

"Not worth killing," Leaphorn thought. But someone had killed him, and gone to considerable trouble in doing it. Why so much trouble? Why had Horseman's body been moved? Why had it been left beside the road when it could so easily have been lost forever, buried under the bank of a thousand arroyos or left for the ravens anywhere in twenty-five thousand empty square miles? And *why* had Horseman been killed? Above all, why had he been killed in that peculiar manner?

The question always brought him back to witch-craft. But all of yesterday afternoon and evening, hours of driving from place to place and hours of frustrating questioning of Hand Tremblers, Listen-ers, and Singers—all the practitioners who knew the most about magic—had told him nothing. Only that the Hand Trembler who examined Tsosie had learned in his trance that the witch was a stranger and that the cure must be an Enemy Way. It was not, Leaphorn knew, a ceremonial lightly undertaken. It required two Singers, one for the patient and one at the Stick Receiver's camp, and the Scalp Shooter. In some cases there would also be a team of Tail Sing-ers for the coyote songs, and the seven Black Danc-ers. Even without the special performers, the Singers and the Scalp Shooter would cost the Tsosie family at least $200 in fees. Dozens of sheep would have to be killed to feed the crowds at both camps, and several hundred dollars more would go for the gift exchanges. Leaphorn thought the Tsosie uncles and cousins who would have to help bear this heavy cost would approve the Sing only if they were sure there had been a witching. And how the devil could they be sure if they hadn't identified the witch?

Leaphorn saw smoke rising from the smoke hole of the ceremonial hogan. Sandoval, who had been burning pine and willow bark by the brush shelter,

had collected his ashes and gone into the log building. The fire inside would be to burn sweetgrass,
dodgeweed, rock sage, and grama mixed with crow
and buzzard feathers, producing a sooty substance
to be mixed with the bark ashes and used to blacken
the patient for his attack on the enemy scalp. Over the
fire, Sandoval would be singing the old chants, the old
songs to the Holy People—not prayers of humility or
supplication, and not pleas for forgiveness, but songs
which sought nothing but to restore man's harmony
with all that was elemental.

The sagebrush flats were stirring with activity
now. A horse race was being organized behind an
array of parked pickups. There will be gambling on
that, Leaphorn thought, and maybe a fight. Cook
fires were burning everywhere. By the hogans, the
women of the family were preparing the ceremonial
food, which two girls would soon take out to provide
the ritual meal for those coming from the other camp.
Leaphorn felt a sudden fierce pride in The People. He
remembered the Blessing Way held when he and his
cousins had left after their last furlough for Camp
Pendleton and then for Saigon and Okinawa.

He remembered the sweat bath and the Singer,
even older than Sandoval, sprinkling his shoulders
with the sacred pollen, and the old, cracked voice rising over the rhythm of the pot drum.

"In the house made of dawn,
in the house made of the evening twilight,
in the house made of dark cloud,
happily may he walk.
In beauty may he walk,
with beauty above him, he walks
with beauty all around him, he walks
with beauty it is finished,
with beauty it is finished."

Leaphorn was sleepy now. The horse race had been
run and won by a boy on a pinto, amid much loud
laughter. A small bare-bottomed boy had walked by
the carryall, smiled shyly at Leaphorn, and relieved
himself in the sage nearby. A dozen or more women,
with their families fed for the morning, were gossip-
ing raucously around an old and rusty sedan. Three
teen-aged girls had led a string of wagon horses down
to the spring, watered them, and put them back on
the picket rope. The sky was cloudless now but light
blue and hazy on the horizons. Later the thunder-
clouds would be building up and there would be
showers—at least over the mountains. Leaphorn
saw the two messenger girls lope away carrying the
ritual food baskets tied to their saddles. A moment
later to the north he heard a flurry of rifle shots and
a swarm of horsemen appeared over the rim of the
flat, whooping and trailing plumes of dust. Leaphorn

climbed stiffly out of the carryall to watch the En-counter Between the Camps. He glanced at his watch. It was 10:12 A.M.

It was late afternoon before the second serenade had been finished and the gifts exchanged. They had been thrown out to the crowd of visitors—first the sacrificial sack of tobacco thrown through the smoke hole of the hogan and caught by a little girl so skinny that it seemed to Leaphorn that she might blow away if the now-gusty breeze caught in her vo-luminous skirts. The child had run to her mother and been rewarded with a hug, and then three men of Tsosie's family began tossing out the gifts stacked under the brush shelter. There was much scrambling and laughing and some sort of practical joke played on a tall man with a mustache and two long braids hanging down his back. The joke caused an uproar of laughter and knee slapping and even the victim was grinning.

Leaphorn had been talking to a young woman from over near Toadlena and had missed the point of the fun, but he gathered from the shouted remarks that it was bawdy. He had, by now, been talking for almost six hours and had lost all count of the number of people he had questioned. Most of them, like this young Salt Water woman from Toadlena, seemed to know nothing at all about subjects which inter-ested Leaphorn. But he had been able to confirm again beyond any shade of doubt that Horseman had returned to this country after the affair in Gallup and to learn that Billy Nez was at the Stick Carrier's camp. The plump young man with the horn-rimmed glasses had told him that. And Horn Rims had been out looking for a stray mule and had seen Horseman walking along a sheep trail back toward the Luka-chukais. Horseman was his second cousin and he had stopped to talk and had given Horseman some tobacco.

"I think his wife had gone off with somebody and he was coming back to his mother's family," Horn Rims had said. He then explained that Luis was a "worthless son of a bitch." In Navajo, the in-sult came out literally to the effect that Horn Rims' second cousin was a stunted male member of a litter produced by a collie bitch. Navajo is a very precise and unambiguous language and the statement left no question that Horn Rims strongly disapproved of his second cousin. But almost two weeks had passed since Horn Rims had seen Horseman and he had no other information to offer, except that Billy Nez was with the Stick Carrier.

The long afternoon of chatting on the subject of the witch had been even less productive. Leaphorn felt he had fairly well confirmed what Sandoval had implied—that the identity of the witch was

not exactly known. Not known, at least, by name, and family, and clan. Leaphorn's instinct told him that several of the Red Forehead clan he had talked to, mostly kinsmen of Tsosies, or members of their extended "outfit," thought of this witch as a specific person, with a specific face, and shape, and habits. It was nothing he could confirm. Leaphorn was a stranger to this clan and he faced the traditional caution of The People where witchcraft was concerned. He had noticed one man slip his hand into his overalls to finger a sacred shape in the medicine bag tied to his loin cloth. The gesture was typical of what he knew others had felt. How did they know that Leaphorn himself was not a witch? And perhaps seeking those who knew of him to make them his future victims? And yet among the garrulous ones, the gossips, there had been some specific details. Several had said the witch was a man, had indicated he was a tall man; all references to him were on foot, none had him riding a horse. The accounts Leaphorn had collected of the witching incidents were conflicting and overlapping and some were obviously wildly imaginative. But he concluded there probably had been at least two or three persons bothered in addition to Tsosie. He had jotted some names in his notebook, but even as he did it he wondered why. The laws he enforced had been taken by the Tribal Council from

the white man's laws and the white man did not recognize witchcraft as an offense.

It would become an offense only if some specified crime was involved. There had been a case of extortion once, nothing they had ever proved, but enough circumstantial evidence to indicate a conspiracy between a Star Gazer and a Singer to diagnose witchings and split fees for the curing ceremonial.

Agnes Tsosie came out of the ceremonial hogan now and went to the brush shelter with a crowd of women relatives and the Singer from the Stick Carrier's camp. Leaphorn saw that one of the women was rubbing tallow on her chin and juniper sap on her forehead. Inside the hogan the same thing would be happening to Tsosie and the other male kinfolks who would be taking part in the attack on the scalp. They would be blackened more thoroughly with the ceremonial ashes, as Monster Slayer had been to make himself invisible before his attack on the Ye-i. If Leaphorn's memory of the ceremonial was correct, Agnes Tsosie would only watch the attack, with a male relative serving as her stand-in during the ritual. The Singer wasn't needed during the blackening and Leaphorn saw Old Man Sandoval talking to the Scalp Shooter, who had been sitting all afternoon beside the hogan entrance, guarding a pile of ashes.

Scalp shooting required a professional, although

his role in the ceremonial was simply to shoot the scalp with an arrow and sprinkle it with symbolic ashes to signify its death. Leaphorn thought he had seen this man before, helping Singers at other ceremonials. He wondered idly what Sandoval was using for the symbolic scalp. Ideally, it would be something from the witch's person, a clipping of hair if that could be had, something with his blood on it, or some article of clothing which had absorbed his sweat. Since this witch was unidentified, the symbolic scalp would have to be something else. Leaphorn guessed they might use a pouch of sand from a footprint or something else they thought the witch had touched.

If it's hair, Leaphorn thought, it's going to mean that Sandoval and some others have been lying. If it was hair or something bloody he would have to confiscate it after the ceremonial ended. He would have the lab check it with Horseman's and, if it matched, have a messy murder investigation on his hands. But he was fairly sure Sandoval hadn't been lying. Linking Horseman to the witching case had never really made sense, never really been more than a faint possibility where no other possibilities were offered. As far as Leaphorn could pin down the witching gossip, Horseman had hardly returned to the Lukachukais when the incidents started, and at least one had happened before the knifing in Gallup. Besides, the

types suspected of witchcraft were always older, usually with a lot of material possessions and a lot of
enemies.

There was the sound of chanting from the ceremonial hogan now, and the thudding of the pot
drum. Sandoval came through the curtain, followed
by Tsosie, two cousins, and the uncle who was repre-
senting Agnes Tsosie. Even their loin cloths had been
blackened with ashes, and each held in his right hand
a raven beak, secured to a juniper stick with yucca
and buckskin thongs. The Scalp Shooter picked up
his basket of ashes and was walking north-northeast.
It was the direction, Leaphorn noted, of the higher
central peaks of the Lukachukais. Over the peaks, a
tremendous thunderhead was rising, its top boiling
in relentless slow motion into the stratosphere, its
bottom black with shadow and trailing the first thin
curtains of rain.

Sandoval will know his medicine is working,
Leaphorn thought. He has called for Thunder to kill
the Wolf and Thunder has come to the appointed
place. It was interesting that the Singer from the
Stick Carrier's camp had placed the scalp so carefully
north-by-northeast of the hogan. That meant they believed the Wolf was now somewhere in that direction.

Leaphorn trailed along with the crowd. The
Scalp Shooter had stopped at a dead creosote bush

about two hundred yards from the hogan and was sprinkling something under the bush with ash. He stepped aside and Tsosie and his kinsmen poked at the object with their raven bills, killing it with this symbol of contempt. Leaphorn pushed through the crowd. The spectators were silent now and he could hear the attackers muttering, "It is dead. It is dead," each time they struck the symbolic scalp.

The object the crowbills were striking was a high-crowned black hat.

Instantly, Leaphorn correlated this new fact with other information, with the bulky stranger trying on hats in Shoemaker's, with the question of why a worthless hat would be stolen and a valuable silver concho band left behind.

The hat was thoroughly coated with ashes now, but there was still a dark outline against the faded felt, the outline of linked circles where heavy silver conchos had once protected the dye from the sun.

When I look in the hatband, Leaphorn thought, it will be size seven and three-eighths. The Big Navajo was the Navajo Wolf. But why was he the witch? This was why the Hand Trembler and Sandoval had decided to prescribe an Enemy Way. The Navajo Wolf was a man nobody knew. A stranger to the clan and to the entire linked-clan society of the Lukachukai slopes. But what had he done to be singled out for this terrible proscription of The People? Death within the year by his own witchcraft—turned against him by the medicine of the Enemy Way. Or, Leaphorn thought grimly, death much sooner if the Tsosies or the Nez family happen to catch him.

The high slopes of the Lukachukais were obscured now by the darkness of the cloud. Light from the setting sun glittered from the strata of ice crystals forming in the thin, frigid air at its upper levels. Deep within it, the structure of the cloud was lit by a sudden flare of sheet lightning. And then there was a single lightning bolt, an abrupt vivid streak of white light pulsing an electric moment against the black of the rain, connecting cloud and mountain slope.

If the witch was there, he's dead enough, Leaphorn thought. And he couldn't blame himself for that. Not the way he would blame himself if The People found the Wolf before he did and executed this sentence of death.

11

There had been intermittent thunder for several minutes. But, even so prepared, McKee had been startled by the sudden brighter-than-day flash of the lightning bolt. The explosion of thunder had followed it almost instantly, setting off a racketing barrage of echoes cannonading from the canyon cliffs. The light breeze, shifting suddenly down canyon, carried the faintly acrid smell of ozone released by the electrical charge and the perfume of dampened dust and rain-struck grass.

It filled McKee's nostrils with nostalgia. There was none of the odor of steaming asphalt, dissolving dirt, and exhaust fumes trapped in humidity which marked an urban rain. It was the smell of a country childhood, all the more evocative because it had been forgotten. And for the moment McKee dismissed the irritation of J. R. Canfield and reveled mentally in happy recollections of Nebraska, of cornfields, and of days when dreams still seemed real and plausible. Then a splatter of rain hit; big, cold, high-velocity drops sent him running to the tent for his raincoat and back out into the sudden shower to rescue the eggs frying on the butane stove and bedrolls spread out on the sand beside a jumble of boulders.

When he reached them the rain stopped as abruptly as it had begun. McKee dropped Canfield's blankets and cautiously inspected the slice of sky visible above the canyon. Up canyon it was blue-black, with a continuing intermittent rumble of thunder. Directly overhead, the clouds were a mixture of gray and white. Down canyon to the south and east there was the dark blue of open sky and, nearer the horizon, the violent reds and yellows of the setting sun. The breeze had shifted back to the southwest now and he saw the rain was drifting across the canyon higher in the mountains. Only the trailing edge of it had touched here.

McKee decided it would be safe to leave the bedrolls out. He walked back to the butane cooker, forked an egg onto a piece of bread and folded it into a sandwich. The sunset now was flooding the canyon with eerie rose light, which made the eroded sandstone and granite of the cliff seem to glow. McKee heard the water then, a small sound, moving down the canyon floor below him. The rain had been little more than a heavy sprinkle here but northwestward on the mesa it had been heavy enough to send runoff down the network of washes which fed Many Ruins Canyon. It would have to rise into a torrent eight or ten feet deep before it topped the high mound of talus where the camp was and McKee estimated the stream, now spreading across the flat sand on the canyon bed below him, was no more than six inches deep. It was muddy, carrying a burden of sticks, pine needles, and assorted debris, but it wouldn't get much deeper unless the rain upstream turned into something like a cloudburst. If that happened, it might be a little tough driving on the canyon bottom tomorrow. That turned McKee's thoughts again to Canfield.

Ever since his return to the camp he had alternated between uneasy worry that some inconceivable something had led Canfield to sign a false name to his note, irritation at himself for such foolishness, and then irritation at Canfield for causing this uneasiness. He was all the more irked by the thought that, when Canfield returned and explained the signature had been inspired by some ridiculous Canfieldian whim, the whole affair would seem too asinine and trivial for complaint.

"Silly bastard," McKee muttered. He folded the third egg into a sandwich, poured himself a mug of coffee, and scrubbed out the frying pan with sand. By now the light in the canyon had faded from rose to dusky red and McKee's mood had shifted with it, back to irritation with himself for being nervous.

It was about ten when he finished going through his accumulation of notes in the tent and planning his activities for the next day. He would have to stay in camp at least until Canfield returned because tomorrow Miss Leon was supposed to arrive. If Canfield was finding anything interesting in his digging, he wouldn't want to stop—and someone should take the girl up into the labyrinth of canyons to try to locate the van truck. It might, or might not, belong to her electrical engineer, but it shouldn't be too hard to find. Not if it was still parked in Hard Goods Canyon, and not if, as Old Woman Gray Rocks had said, the canyon ran into Many Ruins nine miles up from the mouth. That would make it only about four miles up from their camp.

He turned off the butane lantern and stood at the tent flap a moment, letting his eyes adjust to the night before walking back to the bedrolls. He felt tired now, ready for sleep. He left his boots beside the bedding, rolled his shirt in his trousers for a pillow and slid into the blankets. The storm cloud had drifted away and he heard, far to the northeast, the faint suggestion of thunder. His side of the canyon was in total darkness but the top of the sheer cliff on the west side was tinged now by the dim yellow light of the rising moon. It would be about three-quarters full tonight, McKee thought, and he felt a sudden inexpressible loneliness, a loneliness almost as intense as in a dream he sometimes had. In the dream he floated in a great airy blackness, wanting to shout, but remembering—dream fashion—that he had shouted before and his voice had been lost in an infinite echoless distance. Remembering this would sadden him because it told him there was no one anywhere but him. When he had this dream, sometimes when he was overtired and depressed, it would awaken him and he would sit on the side of his bed and smoke a cigarette, and sometimes two or three.

A whippoorwill sounded its whistling call far down the canyon and was answered by an echo. And then it was eerily silent.

Directly overhead McKee picked out the stars of the Pleiades—six in two parallel rows and the seventh trailing to close the double line. From these, McKee remembered, the seven Hard Flint Boys of the Navajo myth had descended to follow Monster Slayer on his heroic odyssey among the evil things. And to spread their own mischief among the Dinee.

And to receive ceremonial offerings of cornmeal every spring from a thousand sheepherders in a thousand little sacred shrines on a thousand mesas and mountains across the Reservation. McKee located two stars, each surrounded by the hazy light of a nebula, which represented the Hard Flint Woman and a contestant in the Bounding Stick Game. He couldn't dredge up the name of the other Holy Person but he vaguely remembered that in the myth there was an argument over the outcome and a solution based on the trickery so inevitable in both Greek and Navajo myth. Far up the west rim of the canyon, a coyote yipped twice, and then poured out its soul in a full-throated bay. The sound seemed to float down from the stars, the voice of some primeval hound drifting infinite sorrow across the sky.

It might be my coyote, McKee thought, the one that got into Yazzie's ram pen. He would go back tomorrow to find out how, if his guide duties with Miss Leon allowed. He shifted his weight on the packed sand and felt suddenly less sure that he would find any way a coyote could have invaded that tight little enclosure. In this silent darkness mystery seemed suddenly natural, almost rational. Down the canyon the whippoorwill called again and then there was the odd, rasping cry of a saw-whet owl, sounding, McKee thought, like an ogre filing off his chains. He reached for his cigarette pack, decided against it, and thought again of the note Canfield had left, and why Jeremy Robert Canfield, whose first name was part of a private anthropology faculty joke, would sign "John" to this note. He drifted uneasily on the margin of sleep.

The sound jerked him abruptly up from the blankets, wide awake, staring across the canyon. It had been the clatter of a falling pebble, bouncing down the eroded cliff and dislodging a small shower of other pebbles. The residue of faint echoes lingered a second in the stillness and then faded. McKee sat stock-still, listening, feeling the tenseness of muscle fiber flooded with adrenalin and the taste of primitive fear in his mouth. He slid his legs out of the bedroll and slipped them into his trousers, put on his boots, picked up his shirt, and stood. The moon had risen halfway up the sky and the west wall of the canyon was flooded now with pale light. McKee stood in a rigid crouch, listening, studying the worn outcroppings of sandstone from which the sound had come. There was nothing but the silence. A sinister shape half hidden by juniper at the foot of the outcrop became, as McKee's eyes better adjusted to the half light, an oddly eroded boulder. McKee relaxed slightly, feeling the panic leaving him. It could have been an animal. And, as he thought this, it seemed ridiculous to think it could be anything but

an animal—perhaps a night-prowling porcupine.
He stood there, feeling suddenly slightly weak and
very foolish. But still there was something primitive
within his mind signaling danger and urging caution. Five black rams with bloody throats and the
wrong name signed to a simple note. A burrowing
owl glided slowly down the moonlit side of the canyon floor, scouting for night-feeding kangaroo rats. It
swerved suddenly away from the outcrop, flapped its
wings wildly, and disappeared in the darkness down
canyon from McKee. And, as it disappeared, his fear
returned. Something had startled the owl. It would
not have been frightened by anything small.

He moved cautiously away from the bedroll, farther back into the darkness up the talus slope toward
the east cliff, taking each step carefully, climbing
slowly over the smaller boulders, carefully skirting
the larger ones. In a pocket of water-cut rock directly
under the overhanging cliff he stopped and turned
back to look behind him, surprised that he was pant-
ing from the brief exertion and fighting to keep his
breathing silent.

The light of the climbing moon had moved halfway across the canyon floor. Nothing stirred. The
canyon was a crevice of immense, motionless, brood-
ing quiet. McKee studied the outcropping carefully,
shifted his eyes slowly down canyon, examining ev-

ery shape under the flat, yellow light, and then examining every shadow. He felt the rough surface of the rock cutting into his knees and started to shift his weight, but again there was the primal urging to caution. It was then he caught the motion.

Something in the black shadow behind the outcrop had moved slightly. McKee stared until his eyes burned, rubbed them, and then stared again. And he saw the dog's head. It inched slowly out of the shadow into the moonlight. First a muzzle and then the head, its ears upright and—McKee strained his eyes until he was sure—its mouth hanging unnaturally open. The head remained there, motionless. McKee stared, every muscle rigid. The dog's head seemed unnaturally high—unless, McKee thought, it was standing on some sort of ledge behind the outcropping. And then there was motion again.

The dog became a man. A large man with the skin of a wolf over his shoulders, its empty skull atop his own head. He moved across a patch of moonlight and disappeared behind a growth of bushes at a foot of the west cliff talus. When the shape reappeared a moment later, McKee thought for a split second that his eyes had been deceiving him—that it actually was a wolf. But it was a man, running in a crouch across the damp sand of the canyon bottom, running with silent swiftness directly toward McKee's tent. The man held something in his right hand, something perhaps a foot long, metal which reflected the moonlight. It was a long-barreled pistol, with an ammunition clip jutting down in front of the trigger. A machine pistol.

The shape disappeared again, out of sight behind the talus slope on McKee's side of the canyon. McKee bent and felt around his feet for a rock, selected one about the size of a softball. When he raised his head, the figure was back in view—in the shadow but silhouetted now against the moonlit cliff. McKee gripped the stone and watched. The panic was gone now, replaced by a kind of grim anger. The figure was at the tent, standing motionless. Listening, McKee thought. Listening and not hearing a damned thing and wondering about it. Then the shape was gone, out of sight behind the tent. McKee had almost decided the man had somehow slipped away when he saw him again, by the bedrolls now, but brush and boulders obscured the area and he couldn't see what the man was doing. He studied the cliff wall on both sides of his pocket. He could climb out of this sheltered place by working his way past a huge block of sandstone just beside him. He could probably make his way down canyon without being in view from the camp.

But if he comes this way, McKee thought, this might be the best place to face him. I could probably knock him down with my rock before he saw me. Unless he has a flashlight as well as the gun. Then there wouldn't be much chance.

And, while he thought this, the utter irrationality of it all occurred to him. It was unreal. Like some crazy childhood nightmare.

But the man was there, real enough, back by the tent now and no longer seeming to make any effort at concealment. He raised the hood of McKee's truck and McKee had a sudden wild hope that he would start it, climb in, and race away, nothing more than a thief. Instead, he closed the hood and walked back and into the tent. A moment later a spot of light showed through the canvas. The flashlight beam shifted, held steady, shifted again, and then stopped. He's looking through my papers, McKee thought. He wondered what the man would make of his notes on the witchcraft interviews. And he had a sudden impulse to walk into the tent, confront the man, and demand to know what the devil he was doing. Then the light snapped off and the man appeared again in front of the tent, staring almost directly toward McKee's hiding place. McKee felt the impulse die.

"Doctor McKee?"

The man called in an even, sonorous voice, not much above a conversational tone. But in the stillness the sound seemed obscenely loud. And the canyon walls said "Kee-Kee-Kee" in a receding echo of his name.

"Bergen McKee," the voice repeated. "I need to . . ." The echoes drowned the rest of it. "I need to talk to you about Doctor Canfield," the voice said. And the man stood silent until the echoes died again. Who is he? McKee wondered. The Navajo bitten by the snake? Or was this man a Navajo? He couldn't tell anything from the voice. There was no trace of accent. But then educated Navajos rarely had accents, except for sometimes dropping the "th" sound.

The man stood silent a long moment, staring up, and then down, the canyon. Listening. And he won't hear a damn thing, McKee thought. Not from me.

"John's hurt," the voice said. The voice was louder now and the cliffs bounced the "hurt" between them until it blended into a single note. "He needs help."

John. John, not Jeremy. The man standing down there in the darkness, the man with the wolf skin, the man who had stalked like an animal, had some connection with Canfield's note, with Canfield's peculiar signature.

"I should go down there," McKee thought, but he remembered the thing that had reflected the moonlight in this man's hand as he had crossed the canyon floor. Why the pistol? Why the dog skin? And he leaned motionless against the boulder, feeling the rough coldness of the rock against his legs and the cold sweat on his palms, knowing he would go nowhere near this man. Not alone in this dark canyon. Not without a weapon.

And then the man was gone. Suddenly he was no longer beside the tent. And then McKee saw him, trotting diagonally across the canyon bottom, the wolf skin dangling from one hand.

McKee relaxed against the boulder, suddenly aware that he was cold and that his shirt was wet with sweat. Far down canyon the saw-whet owl made its strange, rasping cry. Signaling a kill, McKee thought.

12

It was well after midnight when Leaphorn finally learned who had collected the scalp for the ceremonial. He had talked until he was tired of talking—tired and frustrated and irritated at his close-mouthed people. And then a girl had told him, proudly and without prompting, that Billy Nez— whom he still hadn't located—had stolen the hat. Billy Nez had tracked the truck of the witch and had watched from hiding until he finally had the opportunity. Leaphorn had been captured by the girl, a plump and pretty youngster wearing a T-shirt with "Chinle High School" printed across it, during the Girl Dance. She had grabbed his arm while he was talking to an old man.

"Come on, Blue Policeman," she had said. "I've got you and you've got to dance." And Leaphorn had let her tow him to the great fire, because he had already decided the old man would tell him nothing, and because it was the tradition at this ceremonial. He would dance with the girl a little, and after a while he would pay her the proper ransom for his release, and then he would continue wandering through the crowd asking for Billy Nez but no longer really expecting to find him here.

Blue Policeman, he thought. A hell of a lot of good it does to leave your uniform at home. There's not an adult at this Sing by now who doesn't know I'm the law.

The chant rose in the firelight. Ya Ha He Ya Na He. Rising and falling with the rhythm of the pot drums. And then the words. "Lie closer to me," the singers chanted. "Bring your sheepskin and we will go into the darkness. What are you going to do out there?" Leaphorn glanced at his partner, curious whether the ribald suggestion of the song would embarrass a boarding-school girl. She danced gracefully, gripping his left arm with her right.

"I wonder why Hosteen Policeman looks at me," she said. "Are you going to arrest me?"

Leaphorn returned the smile. "I would if I thought you could tell me anything."

"Who are you after? What do you want to know?"

"I'd like to know all about a witch," Leaphorn said.

"I'll bet you don't even believe in witches."

"I believe in a witch who used to wear a big black Stetson hat until somebody got it away from him."

"That was Billy Nez," the girl had said. There it was, as simple as that. Billy Nez was around here somewhere (the girl glanced over her shoulder into the darkness, frowning).

"I'd like to talk to Hosteen Nez," Leaphorn said.

"So would I. I caught him and made him dance and he just paid me twenty-five cents. And he said he'd let me catch him again." The girl frowned into the darkness again and then looked up at Leaphorn. "But he's no Hosteen yet. He's just a boy."

"How old is just a boy?"

"He's just sixteen."

And you're about fifteen, Leaphorn thought, and if Billy Nez isn't careful his clan is going to lose itself a boy, and a bride's price to boot.

"Just a boy," Leaphorn said.

"But he's the one who got the hat. Billy was the Scalp Carrier. He followed that man's pickup, and he watched from where the witch couldn't see him, and when he went away Billy was the one who got the scalp."

And that seemed to be exactly all the girl knew

about it. She knew Nez was Red Forehead, and that he raised sheep with his uncle over on Cottonwood Flats near Chinle, and that he was wearing a red-checked shirt and a red baseball cap, and some of the other things that fifteen-year-old girls learn about sixteen-year-old boys. And then suddenly the pot drums and the chanting stopped, and there was much haggling and laughing and banter as the women collected their ransom fees. Leaphorn gave the girl a dollar.

"That's the most I got all night," she said. But she wouldn't come with him to point out Nez.

Leaphorn spotted the Carrier of the Scalp a half hour later. The Sway Dancing had started then and he saw Nez in his ball cap among the line of dancers from the Stick Receiver's camp. The rhythm was faster now and the rising, falling sound of the voices was as old as the earth. But the words were about a rocket.

"Belacani's rocket fell on the mesa," the singers chanted.

And then the line of men from the patient's camp began the rhythmic swaying and the words changed.

"Belacani's rocket start the brush burning."

Track down the man who started that one, Leaphorn thought, and you'd find the missile the Army spent half the winter looking for four years ago. Trouble was it would be easier to find the missile than the song writer.

But he had, at least, found Billy Nez, and now the dancing was over for a time and Nez was walking toward him, talking to a younger boy who, Leaphorn guessed, would be his cousin.

"My nephew," Leaphorn said, "I would like to talk for a moment with the man who carried the scalp."

Billy Nez looked surprised and pleased. But, Leaphorn noticed, he also moved his hand toward his shirt front to touch his medicine pouch with its gallstone proof against witches. One was careful of strangers at an Enemy Way.

"I myself am a policeman," Leaphorn said. "It is sometimes my business to track people and it would be good for me to hear how you tracked this Wolf."

The boy looked down. "It was nothing very much," he said. And then, remembering his manners, added, "My uncle." For the first time in a long day, Leaphorn felt he was handling someone exactly right.

"And yet nobody else got the scalp for this Sing. It was you, Hosteen Nez."

"Billy tracked him three days," the younger boy said. He grinned at Leaphorn. "I'm Billy's uncle's son."

"We might sit here by this pickup and smoke," Leaphorn said. He took a cigarette and handed the pack to the younger boy. And when the pack came to Billy Nez he took a cigarette, and lit it, and told Joe Leaphorn everything he knew. And he started, as Leaphorn knew he would start, from the beginning.

The witch had first come around the summer hogans of his uncle at mid-spring not long after his uncle's family had driven the sheep up from the winter grazing in the Chinle Valley to the summer range in the Lukachukais.

Two days after they had settled down, he and the two boys were driving the sheep up there on the plateau. His uncle was driving his own sheep and the boys were driving his uncle's wife's sheep. And they saw this truck coming across this arroyo there. It wasn't really a truck. More like a jeep, only bigger and with a cloth top on it.

"Was it a Land-Rover?" Leaphorn said.

"I don't know," Billy Nez said. "I never saw another one like it. It was gray."

The Big Navajo had left Shoemaker's store in a Land-Rover, Leaphorn thought. Gray and hard to see and I wonder if that's a coincidence.

The truck had stopped at first and his uncle had seen the driver looking at them. And then it drove up and the man asked my uncle where he was taking those sheep and how long he was going to keep them in that high country. His uncle had said all summer and the man had asked if he didn't know there was a witch cave up in that country and a bunch of wolves up there that got after people that came into their territory.

Billy Nez took a long drag on his cigarette, inhaled, and then blew out the smoke.

"What'd your uncle say?" Leaphorn asked, and was instantly irked with himself for his impatience.

"He thought it was kind of funny this Nakai knowing so much about Navajo Wolves."

Leaphorn looked at Billy Nez sharply.

"Why Nakai? Did your uncle think this man was a Mexican?"

"Mexican, or Belacana, or something," Billy Nez said. "Anyhow my uncle said he didn't talk much good Navajo. Wanted to talk in English and my uncle don't talk that much, so he tried to talk in Spanish and this man didn't know that good." Billy Nez paused. "So I guess he wasn't a Nakai, come to think of it. Maybe a Ute or something."

So, Leaphorn thought. No doubt now why the Hand Trembler had prescribed the Enemy Way instead of the Prostitution Way. Here's why they thought the witch was a foreigner—an enemy ghost to be exorcised. But the man in the Land-Rover, the man with the black hat, had been a Navajo. Leaphorn was certain of it.

Anyway, Billy Nez was saying, his uncle had said he didn't pay much attention to witches when he needed grass for his sheep and the sheep of his wife, and the man had driven away. But after that his uncle had known something was going to be wrong.

The first week they were back in the high country a young coyote had trailed his uncle, followed his horse all the way across the mesa one morning. That was the Coyote People telling him to watch out. The Coyote People caused a lot of trouble, Billy Nez said, but they were good about warning people.

A little bit after that, at night, his uncle heard the Wolf on top of his hogan. Some dirt had fallen down from the roof on the east side of the hogan (and now, Leaphorn thought, the other three compass points), and then on the south side, and then on the west side and then some dirt fell down on the north side. And then his uncle had known the Wolf would be looking down the smoke hole to see where they were and to blow some corpse powder down on them. But the uncle of Billy Nez was not afraid of a Wolf. He ran outside the hogan to chase him away but he didn't see anything for sure. Maybe he saw a dog running away but he wasn't sure.

"That would have been about the first part of May?" Leaphorn asked.

"A little bit before that," Billy Nez said. "The

moon was in its last quarter two cycles so it would have been in the last part of April."

Almost two weeks before Luis Horseman came home to die.

But the second time his uncle had seen the Wolf. It was daylight then, sundown but still daylight, and his uncle was bringing some of the sheep in for watering and he had thought something was watching him maybe. He looked up to the rim of the mesa and there was this witch standing there, looking at him. He was up on the mesa rim on the rocks with this wolf skin on him, but his uncle could tell it was a man. His uncle had said this witch had stood there looking at him and then made some medicine with his hands. His uncle had thought he might be calling to the other witches to come out of their cave and help. His uncle drove the sheep down to the hogan and they sprinkled pollen and sang the songs from the Night Way. The songs against witches.

"What day was that?"

"That was three or four days after the first time on the roof," Billy Nez said. "I think it was three days."

After that, his uncle had taken his .30–30 with him when he herded the sheep and he had left one of the boys at the Hogan with his wife, in case the witch would come there while he was gone. And he thought he had better track this Wolf and kill it. He went up on the mesa where he had seen the Wolf, and he found tracks there. Some of them were big boot tracks and some were like a big dog. It was still the Season When the Thunder Sleeps and the ground was damp from the snow thaw and tracking was easy.

"My father is a brave man," said the cousin of Billy Nez, and was instantly embarrassed by his rudeness. They smoked a moment in silence to let the incident pass. Then Billy Nez resumed his story.

Under the other slope of the mesa, his uncle had found tire tracks. The Wolf had driven up there and left his truck and then come back to it and driven away. After that the Wolf had started bothering the live-stock. That first night, his uncle had heard the horses whinnying like they were scared and then he heard one of them screaming, and when he ran out there to where he had them penned, two of them had their tendons cut and his uncle had to kill them.

Leaphorn raised a hand in interruption. This surprised him. He had expected nothing so concrete.

"My nephew, did you see these horses?"

"I saw them. The Wolf must have done it with a hand ax. He cut both of the rear tendons on the mare and he hit the colt so hard that it broke his legbone."

Good enough, thought Leaphorn. I've got another reason for finding this son of a bitch. The

Tribal Council had a law against cruelty to animals. Besides, Leaphorn didn't like a man who would do that to a horse.

After that, Billy Nez continued, it was the sheep. His uncle lay out all night with his .30–30 but the Wolf didn't come back anymore for a while. And then the moon came and one white night he heard some rifle shots and he ran out there and the witch had been shooting into where the flock was sleeping. Three of them were dead and he had to butcher some of the others that were hurt.

"After that my uncle talked about it with my aunt and they decided to bring those sheep out of there. They didn't think they could catch that witch and he might get them. So they came on down here."

Leaphorn passed around his cigarette pack again.

"When was it he shot those sheep?"

"Night just like this," Billy Nez said. He looked at the moon, which was two nights short of full phase.

"Be about twenty-six, twenty-seven days ago. One moon back."

"And when did you go after the witch?" Leaphorn asked.

"Well, my uncle's father came over to our place with some of the other men of the outfit and they talked it over. And then they got that Hand Trembler in and he sang the hand-trembling songs and held his arm out over my uncle and it shook and shook. He said the reason he'd been having these dreams was this foreign witch was bothering him."

Billy Nez took another deep drag on the cigarette.

"Or maybe it was the ghost of the witch. Anyway, after that they tried it out by having a blackening. My uncle slept that night with the ashes on him and he didn't have any dreams, so they decided the Hand Trembler was right. The ghost couldn't find him with those ashes on him. So the next night they got together again there in our hogan and decided they ought to find a Singer who knew the Enemy Way."

Billy Nez paused again.

"And my cousin told them he would find the Wolf and carry the scalp," the younger boy said.

"My grandfather didn't want me to do it. He said it was supposed to be an older man who got the scalp. Somebody who'd had an Enemy Way sung over him. But finally they said I could do it."

"You know the Tracking Bear Song?" Leaphorn asked.

"My grandfather taught me that," Billy Nez said. He laid his cigarette on the ground and chanted softly:

"In shoes of dark flint I track the Ute warrior,
In armor of flint I slay the Ute enemy.

With Big Snake Man I go, tracking the warrior.
I usually slay the Ute men and slay the Ute
women.
Tracking Bear I go, taking Ute scalps."

Billy Nez stopped, suddenly embarrassed, and recovered his cigarette.

The three sat in silence a long moment. The chanting had started at the fire again, another sway dance. This time the song was old, a pattern of rhythmic monosyllables which had lost coherent meaning somewhere in time.

"How did you know where to look for the scalp?" Leaphorn asked.

That had taken time, Billy Nez said. His uncle had drawn for him the way the tracks of that truck had looked.

"Like this," Billy Nez said. He smoothed the bare earth with his palm and opened his pocket knife.

"The front tires had a track like this." He drew the tread pattern in the earth. "And the outside of the track, it wasn't as deep. Like he needed a front end job on his truck. Tires wearing on the outside. And the back tires were like this." He drew the pattern of high-traction mud treads. "Cut real deep. I thought I could find them."

"And I guess you did," Leaphorn said.

It had taken Billy Nez almost a week. Three hard days on a horse before he had picked up the first of the tracks—old ones, already almost erased by the wind. On the fourth day, he had caught a glimpse of the Land-Rover. He had been on Talking Rock Mesa and had seen it moving down a wash into the Kam Bimghi Valley. After sunrise the next day he found where the witch was working—clearing a track for his truck up the sloping backside of Ceniza Mesa. And, later that day, he had made his scalp coup.

"I left my horse hobbled up there on top," Billy Nez said, "and I hid out there in the rocks, down near where he was working. He was rolling those rocks out of the way and cutting brush to clear the track. Finally he stopped a while and sat down under a piñon there and ate some stuff and some canned peaches and threw away the can. I thought maybe I'd get that can he'd ate out of for the scalp but that wouldn't be very good and so later on I got the hat."

"Tell how you got it," the younger cousin urged.

"Well, along later in the afternoon the clouds built up the way they do and it got shady and the wind got up. He was wrestling with those rocks and his hat kept blowing off. So the next time he moved that truck farther up the slope, he left that hat there on the seat of the truck. When he was working again, I slipped up there and got it."

"And took off the hatband and left it behind," Leaphorn said.

Billy Nez looked surprised. "Yeh. It was silver conchos."

"There was a rifle there in the truck," younger cousin said.

"Think it was a Remington," Billy Nez said. "Had a long barrel and a telescopic sight. Looked like a .30–06 deer rifle."

"Anything else in there?" Leaphorn asked.

"There was a map folded up there over the dashboard. I think it was a map. And a paper sack on the seat. Maybe part of his lunch. And there was a set of pulleys in the back." The boy paused, thinking.

"A block-and-tackle?" Leaphorn suggested.

"Yes," Nez said.

"Anything else?"

"No. I didn't look much. Just got that hat and then I thought I didn't want to steal that concho band so I took it off. Tied a yucca thong to that hat and tied it on the scalp stick like my grandfather said to do with the scalp—that's so you aren't handling it with your hands so much. And then when I got back up on the mesa away from there, I sang the Tracking Bear Song and used pollen and rode on back to the hogan."

Leaphorn gave the boys each a third cigarette.

"And now," he said, "I want you to tell me

about your brother. I want you to tell about Luis Horseman." He tried to read Billy Nez's face. Was it surprise, or fear, or anger? The boy looked at the tip of the cigarette, and then took a long drag and blew out the smoke.

"I heard Law and Order already found him," Billy Nez said. "I heard Luis Horseman is dead."

"We found his body," Leaphorn said. "He was way down by Ganado when we found him, a hundred miles south of here. We don't know how he got there."

"I don't know," Billy Nez said. "He was staying up there on the plateau between Many Ruins and Horse Fell canyons."

"And you went up there to tell him that he didn't kill that Nakai at Gallup—that the man got well and he should come in and talk to us about it," Leaphorn said. "You did that, didn't you?" His voice was gentle.

"I heard you telling that at Shoemaker's," Billy Nez said. "And I thought you were right. It would be better if Luis Horseman went in to Window Rock and didn't try to run and hide anymore. But when I went up there to tell him and take him some food he was gone."

"That was four days ago," Leaphorn said. "Tuesday. The day I was at Shoemaker's?"

Nez nodded.

"What time did you go? What time did you get there?"

"I waited until it got dark," Billy Nez said. "Luis Horseman told me to do that so nobody would see. But he wasn't there. I got there maybe two hours after midnight and he was gone."

"Blue Policeman," the smaller boy said, "my cousin found something strange there."

"I looked around where he was camping in some rocks and I thought he had taken everything he had with him," Billy Nez said. "And then I looked around some more and I found that the food he had left was buried there—just covered up with sand."

"Were the ashes covered up, too?" Leaphorn asked.

"Covered up with sand and smoothed over."

"Did you see anything else?"

"It was dark. I rode on down into the Chinle Valley and slept until it was light and then I went back up again. Then I found those tracks again."

"The tracks like the Land-Rover left?"

"Same tracks," Billy Nez said. "Up there on the mesa, maybe a half mile from where Luis Horseman was." He paused. "My brother would have taken that food with him. He wouldn't have spoiled it like that."

They sat, smoking in silence.

"I told Luis Horseman that wasn't a good place

to stay. Too many houses of the Old People down in those canyons," Billy Nez said. "Too many ghosts. Nobody likes that country but witches."

The boy was silent again, staring at the fire where the sway dancers were again being moved by the drums in two rhythmic lines.

"I think that Wolf killed my brother," Billy Nez said. His tone was flat, emotionless.

"Listen, my nephew," Leaphorn said. "Listen to me. I think you might be right. But you might be wrong." Leaphorn paused. It would do no good at all to warn this boy against any danger. "This is our business now—Law and Order business. If you hunt this man you would hunt him to kill him and that would be wrong. That man might not be the one who did it. Don't hunt him."

Billy Nez got up and dusted off his jeans.

"I must go now, my uncle, and dance with Chinle High School Girl. Go in beauty."

"Go in beauty," Leaphorn said.

He sat against the truck, thinking about it, sorting out what he knew.

The Dinee, at least the Dinee who lived in the district east of Chinle, thought the Big Navajo was their witch. Billy Nez had found his Land-Rover tracks near Horseman's camp. But they might be old tracks, and they would be gone now. It had rained tonight on the Lukachukai slopes. And the witch, whoever he was, was a violent witch, or a cruel one—a man who would cripple horses with an ax. That was all he knew. That, and the certainty that Billy Nez would be hunting the man who drove the Land-Rover, a danger to the man if he was innocent and a danger to the boy if he was not.

The first sign of paleness was showing at the eastern edge of the night. Soon Charley Tsosie and his wife and sons would come out of the ceremonial hogan. Sandoval would sing the four First Songs and the Coyote Song, and the Tsosies would inhale the required four deep breaths of the air of the Dawn People. Then Charley Tsosie and his people would be cured and the witch who drove the gray Land-Rover and who might, or might not, have maimed two horses with an ax would have his witchcraft turned against him. The Origin Myth gave him one year to live. One year, if the Tsosies or Billy Nez didn't find him first.

13

It was a little more than an hour after daylight when McKee heard the car puttering up the canyon, its exhaust leaving a faint wake of echoes from the cliffs. Canfield had said Miss Leon would be driving a Volkswagen and this sounded like one. It certainly didn't have the throaty roar of whatever it was the man who had stalked him had driven away in the night before.

McKee moved out of the thicket of willows where he had been lying, and prepared himself for a moment he had been dreading. If the car which would soon round the corner ahead was a Volkswagen he would wave it to a stop. If the driver was Miss Leon, she would be confronted with the startling spectacle of a large man with a badly torn shirt, a bruised and

swollen face, and an injured hand, who would tell
her a wild, irrational story of being spooked out of
his bed by a werewolf, and who would order her to
turn around and flee with him out of the canyon.
McKee had thought of this impending confrontation
for hours, ever since it had occurred to him that he
couldn't simply escape from this canyon—and whatever crazy danger it held—and go for help to find
Canfield. To do so would be to leave Miss Leon to face
whatever he was running from.

The car which came around the cliff into view
was a baby-blue Volkswagen sedan, driven by a
young woman with dark hair. McKee trotted down
the slope onto the hard-packed sand, signaling it to
stop.

The Volkswagen slowed. McKee saw the woman
staring at him, her eyes very large. And then, suddenly,
she spun the wheel, the rear wheels spurted sand, and
the car roared past him.

"Miss Leon," McKee screamed. "Stop."

The Volkswagen stopped.

McKee ran to it and pulled at the door. It was
locked. He looked through the window. The girl sat
huddled against the door on the driver's side, frightened eyes in a pale face.

McKee cursed inwardly, tried to pull his gaping
shirt together, and tapped on the window.

"Miss Leon," he said. "I'm Bergen McKee. I was supposed to meet you here. Dr. Canfield and I."

The girl, obviously, couldn't understand him. McKee repeated it all, shouting this time, conscious that the man with the machine pistol must have heard the Volkswagen and might now be taking aim.

The girl leaned across the front seat and pulled up the lock button; McKee was inside in an instant.

"Start turning the car around," McKee ordered. "Head it out of here."

"What's wrong?" Miss Leon said. "Where's Dr. Canfield?"

"Drive," McKee ordered. "Turn it around and drive and I'll explain."

Miss Leon backed the car across the sand, cut the wheel sharply, and pulled the Volks back on the track. McKee opened his door and leaned out, staring back up the canyon. Nothing moved. He looked at Miss Leon, trying to decide how to start.

"What's wrong?" she asked again. "What are we doing?"

She looked less frightened, but now as he turned toward her she saw the bruised side of his face, with the dried blood. Her expression became a mixture of shock and pity.

"I'm Bergen McKee," McKee repeated. He felt immensely foolish. "I'm not sure exactly what's wrong, but I want you to get out of this canyon until I can find out."

Miss Leon looked at him wordlessly, and McKee felt himself flushing.

"I'm sorry I had to give you a scare like that," he said.

"But what in the world is happening? Where's Dr. Canfield? And what happened to your face?"

"I don't know," McKee said. "I mean I don't know where Dr. Canfield is. It's going to be hard to explain it."

He had spent much of his time since daylight planning how he would explain it all, and thinking how ridiculous he must inevitably seem while he tried.

During the night he had worked his way steadily down the canyon, keeping to the rocks close to the canyon wall. When the moon rose directly overhead, flooding the north side of the cliffs with light, he had lain under a growth of brush, resting and listening. And in this silence he had heard the sound of something moving on the rimrock, across the canyon and high above him. Whatever it was—and McKee had no doubt at all that it was the man with the wolf skin—its movements were stealthy. There was not the steady sound of unguarded footsteps on the rock. Only an occasional and very slight noise, with long pauses when there was no sound at all. In those pauses, McKee sensed the man was looking down from the rim, searching the canyon floor and listening for the sound of movement. The feeling was familiar, and less frightening because he had felt it before. Years before, when his company of the First Cavalry had been rearguard in the long, leapfrog retreat down the Korean Peninsula from Seoul toward the Pusan beachhead, he had learned how it felt to be hunted. And, he thought grimly, he had learned how to survive.

The sound had finally moved away from the rim. McKee allowed thirty minutes of silence, and then sprinted across the sand to the south wall. Here the moon's shadow would now fall and here he would be less visible from the rim. He had kept as high on the talus as he could, trading the easier going along the bottom for the invisibility offered by the rocks and brush. He moved steadily, but with infinite caution. His plan was simple. He would travel as far as he could until daylight and then he would find a place from which he could watch the bottom. There he would wait to intercept the car of Miss Leon. He would warn her, get her out of the canyon, send her back to Shoemaker's to get help, and then he would come back to look for Canfield. He no longer had even the faintest hope that the morning would bring Canfield driving up the canyon, safely back from a mercy trip with a snake-bitten Navajo. The sounds on the rimrock had killed that hope. If the motives of the man hunting him were less than sinister he would have been calling for him, not stalking him in silence. And that man, the man with the wolf skin and the pistol, must have stood beside Jeremy as he wrote the note and signed it "John."

He knew my name, McKee had thought. He must have read it in my papers in the tent. He could have learned Canfield's name the same way, but only his initials. And Canfield must have told him the J. was for John and tried, thus, to leave a warning. It occurred to McKee that if the Wolf had taken this trouble to learn who was living in the tent, he would also know of Ellen Leon. Her letter announcing her arrival time was on the table. The Wolf would only have to wait for her.

It had all seemed very obvious in darkness. The man who had stalked him must be insane. There seemed to be no other rational explanation. And this, too, might explain the puzzle of Horseman's murder.

An hour before dawn, when the moon was down and the canyon was almost totally dark, McKee had fallen. A stone shifted under his weight and he had plunged, off balance, eight feet against a slab of rock below. The impact had stunned him for a moment but he was back on his feet before he realized that the little finger on his right hand was pulled from its socket. He noticed its odd immobility before he felt the pain, saw that it was bent grotesquely backward and, when he tried to straighten it, felt the agony of the injured joint. He had sat on the stone then, frightened, trying to listen, to determine if his clumsy fall had alerted the man, but there was a roaring in his ears from the pain. Finally he had gone on, carrying his injured hand inside his shirt. It was then he heard the sound of the motor starting. There was the quick whine of the starter, the sound of a heavy motor, and gears shifting, and then the noise of wheels crunching over a stony surface. The sound came from above, and some distance down canyon. It moved away from him and in a few minutes there was silence again. The man who had stalked him had driven away. He had no way of guessing how far.

McKee had climbed down to the canyon bottom then. Walking was easy on the sand and soon it was dawn. He stopped at a pool where runoff had been trapped in a pocket of rocks. He drank thirstily of the sandy water and then used his left hand to wash as much blood as he could from his face. The skin had been scraped from the right side of his cheek and the bone felt bruised. He rested on a rock and gingerly examined his finger. It seemed to be broken in the knuckle and the tendon pulled loose in his palm. The sky overhead was lightening now and the rocks and trees across the canyon were clearly visible. Night had given way to dawn.

McKee pulled off his left boot and shook out the gravel it had picked up somehow during the night. And then he examined his right hand again. It was a broad hand with strong blunt fingers, two of them crooked. He wiggled the bent knuckle of his first finger and tried to remember how it had felt when he stuck it into that line drive when he was seventeen. He could only remember that it had been swollen for days and that the error had let in two unearned runs.

The distorted knuckle on the second finger was the souvenir of a less serious mishap. He had picked it up in practice where the errors didn't go into the record books. Funny thing about his fielding, McKee thought. Never could learn it. He could hit anybody who ever pitched to him. Bunt and hit to either field, and he had had the power for a kid his age, but finally the coach had used him as a pinch hitter. "Damnit, Berg," the coach had said, "if I leave you out there, you're going to get hit on the head and killed." That had ended his ambitions to be a baseball player, but it still seemed odd to him that the simple skill of timing a grounder and sensing the trajectory of a fly ball had been beyond him. McKee carefully replaced the injured hand in his shirt front. It was throbbing now, but the pain was tolerable. He stood up, surprised at how quickly his leg muscles had stiffened. A mockingbird flew out of a young cottonwood tree, whistling raucously. It was then McKee was suddenly struck with the dismaying thought of Miss Ellen Leon.

Almost certainly in a very few hours he would meet her and, when he did, he would have to make her believe an absolutely incredible story. He walked slowly down the canyon, thinking of how he would tell it. As he thought, the incident seemed first wildly ridiculous and then entirely unreal. The canyon was filled with the cool, gray light of full dawn now. All that had happened under the moonlight was utterly absurd, like something out of a bad melodrama, and his own role in it had been thoroughly unheroic. Yet Miss Leon had to be told—to get her out of the canyon. There simply was no way to explain it all without sounding like a complete fool. McKee wished fervently that the visitor were a man.

He trudged steadily down the canyon, turning in his mind the problem of confronting the woman. He had skipped shaving yesterday in his haste to get to Chinle and call Leaphorn. Now the face which confronted him each morning in his bathroom mirror would be worse by two days' growth of bristles. And the torn and dirty shirt and the scraped cheekbone certainly wouldn't inspire confidence in a female. Neither, he thought glumly, would the improbable tale he had to tell.

When he heard the sound of the motor again, it came almost as a relief. He was crossing the point where a large tributary canyon drained into Many Ruins and where centuries of turbulent runoff had carved the cliffs into a series of horseshoe bends. The motor sound and its confusion of echoes seemed first to come from upstream, and then from downstream. Before it died abruptly away he decided the vehicle might be somewhere up the tributary. Talking Rock Canyon, he thought it was, but he wasn't sure. In the morning sunlight the sound of the truck seemed natural and sane, reassuring him that all that had happened in the darkness had not been merely nightmare.

And now he was sitting beside Miss Leon and she was saying that she wanted very badly to see Dr. Canfield this morning.

McKee converted his embarrassment to irritation.

"Listen," he said. "There's a man somewhere up this canyon who isn't acting rationally. I think he may have done something to Dr. Canfield. I don't know where the hell Canfield is and I can't start looking for him until I get you out of here."

Miss Leon said, "Oh," in a small voice and looked at McKee. He noticed again that she was a very pretty woman.

She thinks I'm a nut, he thought.

"Canfield was gone when I got back to the camp yesterday," McKee went on. "Left me a note and signed it 'John.' His name's Jeremy." Even as he said it, the explanation sounded ridiculous. Miss Leon glanced at him.

"What did the note say?"

"It said a Navajo had come by with a snakebite and he was taking him to Teec Nos Pas." The text of the note now seemed completely reasonable. "But why would he sign it with a phony name?"

"Maybe it was a joke," Miss Leon said.

Maybe it *was* a joke, McKee thought. If it is, I'll kill the smirking bastard.

"I thought of that, too," McKee said. "But last night, sometime after midnight, I saw a man sneaking up on our tent. Had a wolf skin over his head." He had planned not to mention the wolf skin, thinking it might frighten her, or merely make the entire episode seem more ludicrous. But he blurted it out.

"Is that how you got that awful bruise? Did he hit you?"

The sympathy in her voice made McKee feel about seven years old.

"No. No," he said, impatiently. "I fell on a rock."

Miss Leon slowed the Volks and shifted into low gear to make her way across a bed of rocks.

"Your hand's hurt, too," Miss Leon said.

"I'd like you to drive back to Shoemaker's," McKee said. "When you get there, tell Shoemaker that something happened to Canfield and ask him to call Chinle and get the Law and Order boys to send someone in here to help look."

McKee made a wry face.

"Or, if you meet Canfield on your way to Shoemaker's just forget the whole thing." He laughed. "Tell Canfield you met some kind of nut up the canyon named Bergen McKee."

"All right," Miss Leon said. She glanced at the right hand held rigidly inside his shirt front. "How badly . . ."

Immediately ahead of them around an abrupt bend of the canyon, there was the whining sound of a motor running at a high speed.

"Stop a minute," McKee said, but Miss Leon was already braking the car.

As he reached across with his left hand for the door handle, he brushed the injured finger and felt suddenly sick and weak as a fresh wave of pain engulfed his brain. He swung his legs out of the Volks and sat for a moment, head down, while the dizziness passed. He heard Miss Leon opening her door.

"I'll go see what's going on," he said. "You wait here." He realized, with self-disgust, that the words came slowly and his voice was thick. When he got to his feet she was already out of the car. Let it go, he thought. He didn't feel like arguing.

It was less than fifty yards to the canyon bend but McKee had identified the sound before they reached it. He was almost certain it was a winch working. His first glance around the rocky point confirmed this guess. Some five hundred yards downstream the canyon bent sharply to the north through a narrow defile. Here a section of the undercut cliff had collapsed, tumbling huge blocks of rimrock to the canyon floor. Just beyond this pile of talus, McKee saw a gray Land-Rover parked. A cable from the winch reel on its front bumper was attached to a ponderosa pine carried into the canyon by the landslide. The massive trunk of the long-dead tree was being swung slowly across the canyon.

"Looks like we walk out," McKee said softly.

"What in the world is he doing?"

"He's blocking us in with that tree."

"He is, isn't he?" She said it in a very small voice.

McKee couldn't see the man in the Land-Rover very well. He was wearing a black hat and there was something which might be a rifle barrel jutting at an angle out of the side window. The high whining noise of the winching operation had apparently covered the sound of their approach.

"Let's go," McKee said. "We'll drive back up the canyon and find one of those run-in washes, and climb out of here."

The sound of the winch stopped just as they reached the car. There was a long moment of silence as they climbed into the Volkswagen, and then the sound began again. McKee motioned for Miss Leon to start the motor.

"Quietly as you can," he said. "Don't race the motor and get it into second quick as possible."

She said nothing, driving competently and, McKee noticed out of the side of his eye, occasionally biting her lower lip.

"But why would that man want to block the road?" she asked suddenly. "Do you think we should just drive down there and ask him to let us through?"

"I don't think so," McKee said. He felt very, very tired.

"Was that the man you saw last night? The man with the wolf skin?"

"I don't know. I guess it is."

A half mile up the canyon he had her turn off the ignition. From far behind them there still came the high whine of the winch, a faint sound now.

"Anyway, he can't follow us," Miss Leon said. She

smiled at McKee. "He's on the wrong side of his road-block."

"That's right," McKee said. But he knew it wasn't right. He had to work the winch from the down side because the tree top was pointing upstream. He'll simply swing the trunk downstream far enough so he can drive past it and then reattach his winch line from the upstream side and pull it back in place across the canyon. He'll drive in and close the gate behind him. McKee wondered if Land-Rovers had four-wheel drive. He was almost certain they did. The Land-Rover could go anyplace the Volks could go, and lots of places it couldn't. The sense of urgency returned, and his hand and cheekbone began throbbing in harmony.

"Is your hand broken?"

"No," McKee said. "Sprained my little finger."

She looked at him. The sympathy in her eyes embarrassed him and he looked away. "But it hurts a lot," she said. "It would feel better if you let me bandage it."

"I think we better keep going," McKee said. "We'll drive up to our camp and get some water and stuff and find us a place we can climb out of here."

"Maybe Dr. Canfield will be back now," she said. "That is, if he didn't go out to Shoemaker's."

"Maybe so."

She still thinks I'm imagining a lot of this, McKee thought. That was good, in a way. No reason to frighten her more than he already had as long as she would cooperate. And yet it would be easier, somehow, if she shared his knowledge of danger.

Canfield was not at the camp. Nor was there any sign he had been there since McKee had left it. McKee hurriedly filled his canteen. He couldn't find Canfield's. It was probably in the camper truck. His papers were still on the folding table in the tent. If the man had examined them he had taken some care not to disarrange them. He pushed two cans of meat into his pocket, pushed the canteen into the front of his shirt, and picked up a box of crackers. What else would they need? He thought of the can opener on his pocket knife, found it beside his typewriter, and dropped it into his shirt pocket. His pickup, it occurred to him suddenly, would be better than the Volks. They could run it much farther up a side canyon—maybe even get it to the top. He trotted to the truck, switched on the ignition and kicked the starter. Nothing happened. He kicked the starter again and then he remembered seeing the man raising the hood. He raised the hood himself and looked down at the motor. The spark-plug wires were missing. He may be crazy, McKee thought as he trotted back to the Volks, but he's sure efficient.

"O.K.," he told Miss Leon, "we'll drive up the canyon about a mile. There's a place up there we can turn
up a side canyon. We'll drive up it as far as this Volks
will go and then we'll climb out."

Miss Leon was driving very slowly. McKee looked
at her impatiently.

"Better speed it up."

Miss Leon was biting her lip again.

"Dr. McKee. Really. Don't you think we should
wait there at camp?" She looked at him, her face de-
termined. "I'm sure Dr. Canfield will be coming back
soon, and if he doesn't . . . that man we saw down the
canyon, I'm sure that man would help us."

Oh, God, McKee thought. Now I've got trouble
with her.

"You can't possibly climb out of this canyon and
walk all the way back to Shoemaker's with your hand
hurt like that. We're going back."

"Do you know why that pickup of mine wouldn't
start?"

Miss Leon looked at him again.

"Why not?"

"Our friend had pulled the wires off the spark
plugs."

She doesn't believe it, McKee thought. He felt
suddenly dizzy with fatigue and pain.

"Look," he said. "If we had time, I'd take you back

there and show you. But we don't have time." His voice
was fierce. "Now drive and keep driving until I tell
you to turn right."

Miss Leon drove, looking straight ahead. McKee
looked at her profile. Her face was angry, but there
was no sign of fear. It would be better if she was a little
afraid, he thought, and he tried to think of what he
might say. The pain in his hand had become suddenly
like a knife through his knuckles, making concentra-
tion impossible. He inched it carefully out of his shirt
front. The finger was rigid now, turning a bluish color,
and the swelling had spread up the palm to the heel of
his hand. He heard her sudden, sharp intake of breath.

"You need a doctor," Miss Leon said. "That hand's
broken."

McKee put the hand carefully back inside his
shirt, irritated at himself for giving her a chance to
see it.

"It's just a dislocated knuckle. The swelling
makes it look worse than it is."

"This is absolutely insane. I'm going to turn
around and we're going back where you're camped
and soak that hand." She started slowing the Volks.

McKee put his boot on top of her foot on the ac-
celerator and pressed. The little car jerked forward
and she pulled at the wheel to control it.

"Now get this straight," McKee said. His voice

was angry and he spaced the words for emphasis. "I had a hard day yesterday. I was up all night. I'm tired and my hand hurts. I'm worried about Jeremy. You're going to behave and do what you're told. And I'm telling you again that we're going to climb out of this canyon."

"All right, then," Miss Leon said. "Have it your way."

There was a long, strained silence.

"If I'm wrong about that guy, I'll apologize," McKee said. "But really I can't take a chance on being wrong. Not if he's as crazy as I think he is."

Miss Leon was silent. He glanced at her. She looked away. McKee suddenly realized she was crying and the thought dismayed him. He slumped down in the seat, baffled.

"Is this where we turn?"

"Right, up that side canyon."

The tributary seemed narrower now than it had when he and Canfield had poked into it earlier. Just day before yesterday. It seemed like a week.

McKee wondered what he could say. What did you say when you made a woman cry? "Getting pretty narrow," he said.

"Yes."

The canyon bent abruptly and the stream bed here was too narrow for all four wheels. The Volks tilted sharply as the right wheels rolled over a slab of exposed sandstone. It jolted down, slamming the rear bumper against the stone.

McKee suddenly noticed tire tracks on the bank ahead of them. A truck had been in here recently, but before yesterday's rain. Runoff had wiped out the tracks on the sandy bottom but the rain had only softened the imprint where the stream hadn't reached.

McKee was suddenly alert and nervous.

Miss Leon slowed the Volkswagen.

"Do you want me to try to drive over that?" she asked. Just ahead the canyon walls pinched together and water-worn rocks upthrust through the sand.

"I'll take a look," McKee said. He climbed stiffly from the Volks. The rocks were partly obscured by brush and didn't look too formidable. A few yards upstream they gave way to another stretch of sand. Beyond, the canyon rose sharply and was crowded with boulders from a rock slide. It was probably impassable for a vehicle.

"Put it in low and angle to the left," McKee directed. "We can get it past that brush and leave it there out of sight."

The Volks jolted over the rocks more easily than McKee had expected. He showed Miss Leon where to park it out of the water course behind the brush and then collected the canteen and cracker box.

"We can lock the car," he said. "You can take anything you think you'll need, but I'd keep it light."

"I have a box of things I was taking to Dr. Hall," Miss Leon said. "I couldn't replace those."

"We can take it," McKee said. It was then he noticed she was wearing an engagement ring—a ring with an impressive diamond. Why be surprised? he thought. Why be disappointed? Of course she was engaged. Not that it could possibly matter.

Walking was easy for the first fifty yards across the hard-packed sand, but then it became a matter of climbing carefully over the rocks. McKee noticed with surprise that the truck had apparently made it across this barrier. Its path was marked by broken brush. He glanced back. Miss Leon was sitting on a rock, holding her ankle. He noticed she hadn't brought the box.

"What happened?"

"I twisted it." She looked frightened.

He looked at her wordlessly, feeling for the first time in his life absolutely helpless. He walked back down the rocks toward her.

"How bad is it?" He squatted beside her, looking at the ankle. It was a very trim ankle, with no sign yet of swelling.

"I don't know. It hurts."

"Can you put your weight on it?"

"I don't think so."

McKee sat down and rubbed the back of his hand across his forehead. His head ached.

"We'll wait awhile," he said finally. "When it feels better, we'll go on."

He tried to think. If her ankle was sprained, it would swell soon. And if it was sprained it would be almost impossible for her to make the climb out. The long walk across rough country to Shoemaker's would be even more impossible. At least twenty-five miles, he calculated. Perhaps farther from here. What if they simply waited here? Would the man in the Land-Rover follow them? And what if he did? McKee tried to retrace all that had happened since yesterday. The rams with their throats slashed. The note from Canfield. The man who came in the darkness. What had that been in his hand there in the moonlight? Had it really been a pistol? The feeling of being hunted down the canyon. That seemed unreal now. Incredible. But the tree being winched across the canyon had been real. He tried to think of an explanation for it. There was none. It must have been intended to close the canyon behind Miss Leon's Volkswagen. To pen them in. He rubbed his forehead again, and pulled out his cigarettes. Miss Leon was sitting motionless just below him, resting her head on her hand.

She's not very big, he thought. Maybe 110 pounds. If it wasn't for this damned hand he could carry her. Miss Leon's long hair had fallen around her face. Her neck was very slender and very smooth. He felt a sharp, poignant sadness.

"Would you like a cigarette?"

"No thank you," Miss Leon said. She didn't look up.

"I can't tell you how sorry I am," McKee said slowly. "I know you must think I'm out of my mind. But that man . . ." He stopped. There was nothing to be gained by going over it again.

She looked at him then.

"There's no reason for you to be sorry," she said. "I know you're just trying to protect me."

McKee had thought her eyes were black or brown. They were dark blue. He looked away. If he was wrong about this she would forever think of him as the ultimate in idiots. And even if he was right, and she knew he was right, there was her fiancé, the man she was trying so hard to find. And, he realized bleakly, it wouldn't matter anyway.

"But I think we should go back now. We have to go back."

"Maybe so," he said. If she couldn't walk there were no happy alternatives. He would simply have to gamble that he had been insanely wrong about it all. It occurred to him then that Miss Leon might be faking the injured ankle. He didn't think that would be like her. And then he thought about the tire tracks. There had only been one set, which meant the truck had either come out of this canyon before yesterday's rain, or had driven in and parked. A round trip would have left two sets of tracks. He walked up the canyon a few yards to where the brush closed in over the rocks. The branches had obviously been broken by something tearing its way upward. And unless the canyon bottom widened suddenly, and flattened—which looked impossible from here—it couldn't have gone much farther. "I'll be right back," McKee said. "I'm going to see where that truck went."

It proved easy enough to follow. Beyond the barrier of brush, its wheels had straddled the now-narrow streambed, leaving two deep tracks in the loamy soil—tracks which disappeared behind a brush-covered outcropping of rock a hundred feet upstream. McKee walked slowly toward this screen, feeling a growing tenseness. Behind it he would find some sort of vehicle. It couldn't possibly be the Land-Rover. It might be, he realized, Canfield's camper. Or the pickup of some Navajo sheepherder. If it was Canfield's truck, where was Jeremy?

Canfield's camper was parked just behind the outcropping, its front wheels pulled up on a rock slope, tilting it at a sharp angle. McKee stood a moment looking at it. Then he looked up the canyon and stared up at the rimrock above. Nothing was in sight.

"Jeremy?" He kept his voice low.

There was no answer.

The truck was locked. He looked through the side window. No keys in the ignition. But Canfield's hat was on the floorboards. It was a plaid canvas fishing hat, with an oversized feather. A ridiculous hat, but why had Canfield left it behind?

McKee walked to the back of the pickup and peered through the small back window of the camper compartment. Canfield had stripped the interior and used it primarily for weather-proof storage. It was dark inside and McKee could see nothing at first. He pressed his face against the glass and used his left hand as a shield against the reflecting sunlight. He saw, first, a khaki shirt front and then the legs of a man. One was bent sharply at the knee and the other, extended, crossed it at the ankle. The man's head was out of sight, against the tailgate of the camper and directly below the window, outside McKee's line of vision.

He knew instantly that the form was that of Jeremy Canfield and the civilized instincts of his consciousness proclaimed that Canfield was asleep. But some infinitesimal fraction of a second later his reason told him that Jeremy was not asleep. Men did not sleep, head down, on such a steep slope.

McKee tried the handle on the camper again. It
was locked. He looked around him for a rock, wrapped
his left hand in his handkerchief, and smashed at the
glass. It took five blows to force his way through the
laminated safety window. He picked out the shards
of glass still in the way and reached through, un-
snapped the catchlock on the inside, raised the top
panel on its hinges and dropped the tailgate. There
was an outflow of warmer air escaping from the
camper compartment and what had been Dr. J. R.
Canfield slid a few inches toward him.

McKee took a short step backward and stared.
Canfield's mouth was stretched open in some frozen, soundless shout. McKee swallowed and then
sat on the tailgate. With his thumb he gently closed
Canfield's eyes. The eyelids felt sandy under his
touch and he noticed then that there was also sand
around the mouth and in his friend's thinning hair.
He rubbed his hand absently against his pant leg
and stared blindly out across the canyon. He found
himself wondering where Canfield had left his guitar. Back in the tent, he thought. Canfield had been
working on one of his "ethnics" to celebrate the arrival of Miss Leon. McKee tried to remember the
words. They were witty, he recalled, and unusually
unprofane for one of Jeremy's productions. Then
he could think only of Miss Leon, a slight, slender,

weary figure sitting on the rock with her head resting on her arm.

McKee got up, pushed Canfield's body a few inches back up the steep incline of the pickup bed and closed the tailgate. He moved rapidly down the canyon.

There was no alternative now. No question of turning back. But was there a way to get Miss Leon out of this trap without bringing her past this truck? He looked again at the canyon walls. With two good hands he might be able to make it to the top here, but he was sure she couldn't. And he didn't have two good hands. He cursed vehemently as his jogging trot started the throbbing again. If only he hadn't been so clumsy. He would have to bring her past the truck. There was no other way. But he would keep her from looking in.

She was still on the rock when he pushed his way through the bushes, and she looked up and smiled at him.

"We have to go now," he said. "How's the ankle?"

"I don't think I can do more than hobble on it," she said. "We'll have to go back."

"We're not going back. I found Canfield's truck up there. Someone broke in the back window and he's gone."

"But we can't possibly . . ."

"Get up," McKee ordered. His voice was hoarse. "Get on your feet. I'll help you."

"I'm not going," Miss Leon said.

"You're going, and right now." McKee's voice was grim. He gripped her arm and lifted her to her feet, surprised at how light she seemed. The box of crackers was on the rock where he had left it. How could he have been silly enough to bring crackers?

She tried to jerk away from his grip, and then faced him. McKee noticed there were tears in her eyes.

"You've got a concussion. We just can't go stumbling around like this. We've got to get you to a doctor. Please," she said. "Please, Dr. McKee. Please come back to the camp and Dr. Canfield will help you."

McKee looked at her. There was dust on her face and a tear had streaked it. He looked away, feeling baffled and helpless. Maybe he would have to tell her about Canfield.

"Come on," he said. "I'll help you."

"You're hurting my arm."

McKee was suddenly conscious of the feel of her arm under his fingers, of the softness under the shirt sleeve. He jerked his hand away.

Miss Leon ran. She spun away from him and ran lightly down the rocks toward the Volkswagen. McKee stood, too surprised to move, thinking: There's nothing wrong with her ankle. Then he swore, and ran after her, clumsily because of his injured hand. Before he reached the Volkswagen, she had rolled up the windows and locked herself in. For a wild moment, McKee thought she would start the car and drive off and he had a vision of himself trying to keep himself in front of the Volkswagen—performing an idiotic game of dodgem in reverse. But she simply sat behind the wheel, looking at him.

He tapped on the window, and tried to keep his voice sounding normal.

"Really, Miss Leon. I'm not crazy. And we really do have to get out of here."

Miss Leon looked at him. He saw no fear in her expression, nor anger. She simply looked worried.

"Roll down the window."

"Not until you give me your word of honor you'll go back to the camp."

Her voice was faint through the glass.

My day for breaking windows, McKee thought. He picked up a rock, and wrapped the handkerchief around his left hand again. He saw Miss Leon looked frightened now.

"Roll it down."

"No."

McKee hesitated. He thought of Jeremy's body, and of the sand on his face. Breaking his word would be quicker than the window.

"I promise," he said. "Let me in and we'll go back to camp."

"I don't know now," Miss Leon said. "I'm not sure I can trust you."

Good lord, McKee thought. Women left him utterly baffled.

He held up the rock.

"Open up, or I break in."

Miss Leon unlocked the door and he pulled it open.

"Get out now. No more of this horsing around. Get out of there or I'll have to drag you out."

Miss Leon got out. He gripped her arm and walked with her rapidly up the canyon. And then he stopped.

A tall man wearing a new black hat emerged from the screen of bushes just in front of them. He was the Big Navajo who had been shopping in Shoemaker's. In his right hand he held a machine pistol, pointed approximately at McKee's stomach. It was of shiny, gunmetal blue—something which would have reflected in the moonlight.

"That's right," the man said. "Just stand still."

He walked across the rocks toward them, keeping his eyes on McKee.

The pistol, McKee saw, had a wire stock, now folded down, and a long cartridge magazine extending downward from the chamber.

"You're Bergen McKee," the man said. "And the young lady would be Ellen Leon."

McKee pulled Miss Leon's arm, moving her behind him.

"What do you want?"

The man smiled at McKee. It was a pleasant smile. And the face was pleasant. A long, rawboned Navajo face, with heavy eyebrows and a generous mouth. McKee saw he wore short braids, tied with red cord.

"Just the pleasure of your company for a while," the big man said. "But right now I want you to take that hand out of your shirt front, very, very slowly."

McKee pulled out the hand.

"Well," the man said. "I see I've been too suspicious." He smiled again. "That's quite a finger."

McKee said nothing.

"Now, I'll have you put your hands against that tree." He flicked the long barrel of the pistol toward the trunk of a piñon. "Lean against it while I see what you have in those pockets. And, Ellen, you stand over here where I can watch you."

The man stood behind McKee and searched him deftly. He pulled out the cans of meat and dropped them, took the pickup keys and his billfold, ran his hand quickly around McKee's belt line and patted his shirt. Then the hand was gone, but the voice came from directly behind him.

"You will hold that position until I finish checking Miss Leon's possessions. I don't want any movement at all. I don't have to tell you that I will use this pistol."

"No," Bergen said glumly. "You don't."

He heard the voice telling Miss Leon to hold her arms out. McKee looked back over his shoulder.

The blow was so sudden and vicious that he dropped to his knees and huddled against the pain of it. The man had jabbed him, full strength, above the kidney with the muzzle of the pistol.

"You didn't pay attention to what I said," he heard the man saying. "I said not to move. But now you can get up."

McKee pulled himself to his feet. He had hurt his finger again and his hand throbbed violently. He saw Miss Leon looking at him, her face very white. The man was looking at him too, still smiling slightly. He wore a black shirt and denims tucked into the tops of his boots.

"You know, I almost missed you again," the man said. He stopped smiling. "You've been a hell of a lot of trouble. When we have a little time I want you to tell me how you got away from me last night at your camp. That's been puzzling me." The man stopped a moment, staring at McKee.

"I think I know why I didn't catch you at my tree. You were farther down the canyon than I thought you could be and you heard the winch. Didn't you?"

"That's right," McKee said.

"I almost waited there too long," the man said. "You were smart enough to run, but then you gave away your advantage. I wonder why you waited for me here." He looked at McKee thoughtfully. "You could have made me hunt you another day," he said. "Why did you stop? Did you give up?"

McKee didn't look at Miss Leon.

"We didn't think anyone would know where we were."

The Navajo laughed. He seemed genuinely amused. "If you didn't know this was the only way out, I had some luck with you."

"Who the hell are you?" McKee asked. "And what do you want with us?"

"Let's go now. You will walk a little ahead and do as you're told."

He turned the machine pistol sideways, and tapped the safety button beside the trigger guard.

"I carry it cocked, with the safety off. It's a .38 caliber and I'm good with it."

"I'll bet you are," McKee said.

The man kept well behind them as they walked past the brush and over the rocks. McKee walked silently, trying to think.

Miss Leon touched his arm. "I'm sorry." Her voice was very small.

"Nothing to be sorry for."

"If I hadn't been so stupid," she whispered. "I thought it was because you had hurt your head."

"What else could you think? It still seems crazy."

"I'm sorry. You could have gotten away."

"I should have been able to manage it anyway," McKee said. His voice was bitter.

"How did he know our names?"

"He looked through the papers in our tent," McKee said. "I guess he saw them there."

"No talking," the Navajo said. "Save your breath."

They walked in silence up the sand and around the outcropping where Canfield's camper was parked.

"We'll stop here a moment," the man said.

McKee saw Miss Leon looking at the truck. He was glad he had had sense enough to close the tailgate.

"I noticed you looked in it," the man said. "I wish you hadn't broken that window. What did you think that would accomplish? It's going to look funny."

The Navajo moved toward the pickup, watching them as he did. He glanced inside and then briefly inspected the broken window.

"This Canfield seemed like a nice fella," he said. "Full of jokes."

"Then why did you kill him?" McKee asked fiercely. He spoke in Navajo.

The big man looked at him, as if trying to understand the question. He answered in English. "Just bad luck. There wasn't any other way to handle it." He looked at McKee solemnly and pursed his lips. The expression was rueful. "Have to go on now," he said. "It's more than a mile to my car and a lot of climbing."

Within a few hundred yards, the going became increasingly difficult. The canyon floor rose sharply now and was choked by brush and tumbled boulders. McKee climbed stolidly, helping Miss Leon when he could and trying to think. What kind of a monster was this? He seemed perfectly sane, as if this crazy episode were simply business. He had apparently killed Jeremy as unemotionally as he would swat a fly. McKee was absolutely certain he would kill Miss Leon and him with the same coolness. And, as usual, he could do nothing about it. He had thought about turning suddenly and trying to hit the man with a rock. But his right hand was almost useless and the Navajo kept a cautious distance behind them.

It didn't seem likely the man would leave them alive, not with the knowledge that he was a murderer. But why hadn't he simply shot them by the camper? McKee had sensed that the man had considered this, at least for a moment, after he had confirmed that Canfield's body was still in the truck. But he had dropped the idea. He must have some use for us alive,

McKee thought. Either that, or he wants our bodies somewhere else, and it's easier to have us walk. But why? The man seemed sane but there was no conceivable sanity in any of this.

"We'll climb out here," the Navajo said. He indicated a gap in a rockslide which had broken out of the south wall of the canyon. "You go first, Dr. McKee. When you reach the top you will lie down with your feet sticking out over the rim where I can see them. Ellen will be just ahead of me and if you try anything foolish I will have to shoot her so I can come after you. Do you understand how it will work?"

He studied McKee's face.

"You may think I'm bluffing. I'm not. I don't really think I'll need Miss Leon."

McKee looked at her. She stood just below him, breathing heavily from the exertion, her face damp with perspiration. She attempted a smile.

Somehow, McKee thought, I'm going to get her out of this. Even if it kills me.

He began climbing. It was slow because of his right hand, and by the time he reached the top he was drained with exhaustion. He lowered himself onto the rimrock, with his feet jutting out.

"Stay on your stomach," the voice from below ordered.

The position left him completely helpless. He couldn't move without the Navajo seeing him and he had no doubt at all that the man would kill Miss Leon the moment he did. He wondered what the man had meant about probably not needing her. Why would he need her? And why did he need him?

The Navajo reached the top before Miss Leon and stood well aside while she finished the climb.

"Walk right over there to the truck," he said. McKee saw the Land-Rover almost hidden behind a growth of juniper.

"But first hold that hand out so I can see it."

McKee held out his left hand, palm open.

"Are you left-handed, Dr. McKee?"

"No. I'm right-handed."

"I was afraid you would be. Let me see it."

McKee slowly raised his injured hand. He suppressed a wince as motion renewed the pain. The sun was directly south now and that might explain some of the weakness in his legs. It was noon and he hadn't eaten anything since yesterday afternoon.

"That looks bad," the Navajo said. "We may have to soak it to get that swelling down."

McKee saw that Miss Leon was also staring at his hand. He dropped it, flinched again, and the blood drained into it.

"I'm touched by your sympathy," McKee said.

The Navajo chuckled. "It's not really that," he said, grinning at McKee. "It's just that I have to have you write a letter for us."

14

There is no comfortable way, McKee found, to lie face down on the back seat of a moving vehicle with his wrists tied together and roped to his ankles. The best he could arrange involved staring directly at the back of the front seat. By looking out of the right corner of his eye, he could see the back of the Big Navajo's neck. The man had his hat pushed forward on his forehead. That would be because they were driving west and the sun was low through the windshield. By looking down his cheek, he could see Miss Leon, sitting stiffly against the right door of the Land-Rover, as far as she could get from the Indian.

The Land-Rover lurched over something and McKee spread his knees to keep from shifting on the seat. Making the move started the throbbing again in his right hand. The Navajo was saying something but it was lost in dizziness.

"I don't know," Miss Leon said.

"How about you? How long were you planning to stay?"

The question sounded so ordinary and social that McKee had an impulse to laugh. But when Miss Leon had answered two or three days, the Navajo had turned his head toward her. There was a long silence then, and when the Navajo spoke again, McKee realized the question had not been casual at all.

"Did anyone know where you were going?"

"Everyone knew."

"This Dr. Green at Albuquerque knew," the Navajo said. "Who else? What about your husband? Did he know you were coming to this canyon?"

"I don't have a husband."

There was another silence then.

"Who else knew then?" the Navajo asked.

"Some other friends of mine, of course, and my family. Why? What difference does it make?"

"Another thing. Why did McKee sit around in the canyon and let me cut him off?"

"Ask him," Miss Leon said.

"You tell me," the Navajo said.

"Because I was a fool," Miss Leon said.

"You slow him down?" The Navajo chuckled. "Didn't you believe there was a Navajo Wolf?"

"He had that horrible bruise on his forehead," Miss Leon said, "I thought it was that."

"Well, I would have got him anyway."

"No," she said. "If it hadn't been for me, Dr. McKee would have gotten away."

"Maybe you don't know about us Navajo Wolves. We turn ourselves into coyotes, and dogs, bears, foxes, owls, and crows."

McKee stared at the back of the Navajo's head. He had ticked off the litany of were-animals in a voice heavy with sarcasm. And he listed bears, and owls, and crows. There had been a scholarly argument about that when Greersen first published his book about witchcraft beliefs in the 1920's. Greersen had listed only one account of each. The bear story had come out of the Navajo Mountain district and the owl and crow incidents were both far to the east—over on the Checkerboard Reservation in New Mexico. McKee had never found a source who knew of more than were-dogs, were-wolves, and were-coyotes. The big man must have read Greersen, and that had to mean he had researched somewhere with an anthropological library. But why, and where?

"And we fly through the air when it's dark and we

need to," the Navajo was saying. "McKee wouldn't have got away."

"He'd already gotten away once." Miss Leon's voice was angry and insistent. "He outsmarted you last night. And today he outsmarted you again. He . . ."

"Lady. Drop it. You don't know who I am. Nobody gets away."

That had ended the conversation. The Land-Rover had turned sharply and tilted downward—moving mostly in first gear down the narrow bottom of a dry wash. And after what McKee guessed must have been three or four miles there was the feel of smooth flat sand under the wheels and the Navajo drove much faster. There was no sun on the Land-Rover now and McKee was sure they were back on the floor of Many Ruins but he wasn't sure of directions.

A dull pain from the bruise on his forehead and the throbbing of his hand made it difficult to concentrate. Who was the Navajo? In this part of the Reservation, The People linked owls with ghosts, but not with witches, and gave crows and ravens no supernatural significance at all. Obviously, the man's tone was heavily ironic when he listed the birds and animals. McKee could think of no source for such a list except Greersen's *Case Studies in Navajo Ethnographic Aberrations*. It was a notoriously ponderous and difficult volume intended for cultural anthropologists. Why would the Navajo read such a book? When McKee tried to make sense of this, his mind kept turning to the sound of Ellen Leon's voice defending him. "He outsmarted you," she had said.

The Land-Rover stopped and McKee heard the hand brake go on.

"You stay here," the Indian said. "Don't try to untie McKee and don't try anything funny."

And then the door opened, the big man was gone, and Miss Leon was leaning over the back of the seat. She looked dusty, disheveled, very tired, and very sympathetic. "Are you all right?" she asked.

"Where are we? Where did he go?"

"At the tree," Miss Leon said. "The one he pulled across the canyon. Are you all right?"

"What's he doing? Putting on the winch?"

"Yes. Dr. McKee, I'm sorry I was such a silly fool. I didn't . . ."

"I couldn't hear part of the conversation. Did he tell you anything useful? Who he was, or anything like that?"

"No. I don't think so. He said nobody ever got away from him."

"I heard that," McKee said. "Did he say anything else?"

"I can't think of anything." She paused. "He asked me why we waited in the canyon so he could catch us."

"I heard that, too. Don't worry about it."

And then he heard the big man climbing back into the Land-Rover. There was the sound of shifting gears, the whine of the winch, and the cracking noise of limbs breaking. Then the winch stopped and the man climbed out again.

"I want you to be very, very careful," McKee said. "Do exactly what he tells you to do. And keep your eyes open. Watch for a chance to get away. If you can get out of his sight, hide. Hide and don't move until it's pitch dark and then get out of the canyon. Go to Shoemaker's. That's south by southwest of here. You know how to tell your directions at night?"

"Yes," Ellen said.

She probably doesn't, McKee thought, but it seemed entirely academic.

"Find the Big Dipper," McKee said. "The two stars in the line at the end of the cup point to the Pole Star. That's due north."

"He's coming back," she said.

"Remember. Watch for a chance."

And then the big man was leaning over the seat, looking at him. "I hope you were giving Miss Leon good advice."

"I told her to follow orders."

"That's good advice," the Navajo said.

They drove about ten minutes by McKee's estimate before the Land-Rover stopped again.

"This time you better come along, Miss Leon," the man said. "Slide out on my side."

"Where are you taking her?" McKee's voice was loud.

"I won't hurt her," the man said. "We're just going to get some of your papers."

McKee twisted his shoulders and neck, straining to see out the rear window. Only the top of the cliff was in his line of sight, but it was enough to confirm that they were at their camping place.

They were gone only a moment. And then the Land-Rover was moving again, smoothly at first up the sandy floor of Many Ruins and then a jolting, twisting ride. Suddenly they weren't moving. McKee heard the hand brake pulled on.

"I see you got a woman, George. Where's the man you were after?"

The voice was soft. A Virginia accent, McKee thought, or maybe Carolina or Maryland.

"In the back seat," the Navajo said. "Get out, Miss Leon."

The door by McKee's head opened and he saw a man looking down at him. On his stomach, with his head turned to one side, McKee could see only out of the corner of his right eye. He could see a belt buckle, and a navy-blue vest with black buttons, and the bottom of the man's chin and up his nostrils.

"He's tied up," the voice above him said. It seemed to McKee a remarkably stupid thing to say.

"Move a little bit out of the way," the Navajo said. Then McKee felt the Indian's hands, deftly untying the knots.

"Get any calls while you were gone?" the soft voice asked. "Do they know when we can haul out of this hole?"

"No calls," the Big Navajo said. "You see any-thing?"

"No," the soft voice said. "Just that kid on the horse again. Up on the top. Way off across the mesa."

"You can get up now, Dr. McKee."

McKee sat up and examined the man with the blue vest. He was a tall young man with a pale face shaded by a light-blue straw hat. He looked back at McKee and nodded politely—blue eyes under blond eyebrows—and then turned toward Miss Leon.

"How do you do," he said. Ellen Leon ignored him.

The young man wore a harness over his vest sup-porting a shoulder holster with a semiautomatic pistol in it. McKee didn't recognize the type, but it seemed to be about .38 caliber. Miss Leon stood stiffly in front of the truck. She looked frightened.

"Come on," the Big Navajo said. "Get out now. I'm in a hurry."

McKee climbed out of the Land-Rover, his muscles stiff. His head ached, but the ache was lost in the violent throbbing of his injured hand. He held it stiffly at his side and glanced around.

They were up a narrow side canyon. Below, not more than two hundred yards, McKee could see the broad sandy bed of Many Ruins bright in the afternoon sun. Here there was shadow and it was a moment before he noticed the cliff dwelling high on the sandstone wall behind the blond man. It was large for an Anasazi ruin—built in a long horizontal fault cleft some forty feet above the talus slope and protected from above by the sloping overhang of the cliff. He wondered, fleetingly, if it was one of those excavated by the Harvard-Smithsonian teams. It would be hard to reach, but that made it all the more attractive to the archaeologists. Less chance it had been disturbed.

"Dr. McKee is going to write that letter for us, Eddie," the Navajo said. "It may take some time, and while I'm thinking about the letter, you want to be thinking about McKee. He's tricky."

"He hasn't written it yet?" the blond man asked. He sounded surprised.

"I could have had him write it back at his camp," the Indian said. "I think I could handle him. Ninety-nine chances out of a hundred. But why take chances with one this slippery?"

"Too much money involved," Eddie said. "Way too much money for taking chances."

He slipped the pistol deftly from the holster, handling it, McKee noticed glumly, as naturally as a pipe smoker handles a pipe.

"Don't talk so much," the Big Navajo said. "We're going to leave these two behind and the less they hear the better."

Eddie said, "Oh?" The word came out as another question.

The Navajo reached into the Land-Rover, pulled out a pile of papers, stacked them on the hood, sorted swiftly through them, extracted a letter, and skimmed it.

"How about this Dr. Green? Looks like he's your boss. He'd probably be the one to write."

"Green's chairman of the department," McKee said. "We usually try to keep in touch when we're in the field."

How long, McKee wondered, had Canfield lived after he wrote his note for this man? Just long enough for the Navajo to kill him without marks of violence. Only one thing was clear in this incredible situation— the Navajo's need for this letter was all that kept Miss Leon and himself alive. He wouldn't write it, but it had to be handled exactly right.

The Big Navajo handed him Dr. Canfield's ball point pen. It was a slim silver pen, and as McKee accepted it with his left hand he felt his resolution harden. He would never, under any circumstances, write this letter.

"I didn't find any stationery so I guess you used your notebook?"

"That's right," McKee said.

"We'll make it to Dr. Green," the Navajo said. "What do you call him? Dr. Green? Or his first name?"

"Dr. Green," McKee lied. "He's pretty stuffy."

The Navajo looked at him thoughtfully. "What was Dr. Canfield's first name? Was it John?"

"John Robert Canfield," McKee said.

The Big Navajo studied him.

"Dr. McKee," he said finally, "what happened to Dr. Canfield was too bad. It couldn't be helped because Dr. Canfield tried to get away and he didn't leave me any alternative. But there is no reason at all for you and Miss Leon to die. If this letter is written properly it will give us time to finish what we are doing here. And then we will leave and we can afford to leave you behind." He said all this very slowly, watching McKee intently. McKee kept his expression studiously noncommittal.

"You may doubt that, but it's true. When we are finished here, there will be no way at all to trace us. If you cooperate, we can leave you up in that cliff dwelling with food and water. In time, perhaps you could find a way to get down. If not, someone will come in here sooner or later and find you."

"What happens if I don't write the letter?"

The Navajo's expression remained perfectly pleasant.

"Then I'll have to kill you both. Without the letter we'd have to hurry. You would slow us down some, because someone will have to watch you. Nothing personal about it, Dr. McKee. It's simply a matter of money." He smiled. "You know our Origin Myth. That's what witchcraft is all about—the way to make money."

"What do you want me to write?" McKee asked.

"That's part of the problem. We want a letter to Dr. Green telling him that you're leaving this canyon and going somewhere else—somewhere it would be natural for you to go. You and Dr. Canfield and Miss Leon. And it has to be written so that Dr. Green won't suspect anything."

The Big Navajo paused, staring at McKee.

"You can see that, can't you? If someone gets worried and comes in here looking for you, we would simply have to kill you."

I have to do this exactly right, McKee thought.

"I don't think I can believe you," he said. "You killed John after he wrote the letter."

"Your Dr. Canfield was very foolish. He wrote you the note, and then he tried to escape. He jumped me."

"I see," McKee said.

"And I think that Dr. Canfield warned you somehow in that note of his. What was it? Why were you expecting me?"

McKee grinned. "You're right, of course. It was the name. His name's Jeremy. When I saw that signature I knew something was wrong. I'd been over to the Yazzie hogan and found those rams you killed and I was nervous about that anyway."

McKee was satisfied that his voice had sounded natural. He hoped desperately that his timing had been right. Maybe he should have waited longer, but he saw a slight relaxation in the Navajo's face. It's like poker, he thought, and this man's weakness, if he has one, is his vanity.

"You shouldn't try anything like that."

"I don't have any reason to trust you," McKee said. "Just one thing. You kill one man and they hunt for you awhile but it is not so very unusual. You kill two men and a woman and it's something nobody forgets and they keep looking for you."

He was watching the Navajo's face. It relaxed a little more. "You've been thinking of that, haven't you?" McKee asked.

"This is just business with me, Dr. McKee," the Navajo said. "A way to make a lot of money. You're right. The more people who get hurt, the harder they hunt."

With an effort, McKee avoided looking at the blond man. From the corner of his eye, he had seen a faint smile on Eddie's face.

"All right," McKee said. "What do you think we should say?"

"Well. You'll have to say you're leaving here. All of you." He paused. "Say you are leaving day after tomorrow. A day after we mail this at Shoemaker's."

McKee tried to seem thoughtful. "Canfield was looking for Folsom Man artifacts in the Anasazi ruins," he said, aware that the Navajo must already know that. "We'll say he wasn't finding any around here and that I haven't had much luck finding anyone willing to talk about witchcraft incidents."

He glanced up at the Navajo's face.

"If you don't believe that's true, you can send somebody back to get my notes. That really is what I'm working on."

"I believe you," the Navajo said. "Write it here on the hood of the truck."

The son of a bitch read my notes, McKee thought. He felt elated. Then he saw Ellen Leon watching him, her face without expression. The elation died. She thinks I'm a coward or a fool, he thought. Maybe that was best.

"I'll tell Green that we're moving on up into the Monument Valley country in Utah—where the Navajos are less exposed to outside influences and less accultured. That would make sense for both of us. Canfield is . . ." He hesitated a second, sickened at this play-acting. "Canfield was trying to establish some pattern of Folsom Man hunting camps in this area. The early pueblo builders collected Folsom lance points and kept them as totems. That would be a good place for him to be looking."

He was fairly confident that the big man knew all about what both of them were doing, and he tried to make his voice sound persuasive. He doubted if the man knew about Ellen Leon. There was nothing mentioning her in the tent. Just her brief note.

"And it would be a natural place for me to work. In the back country is where you find people still believing in the Navajo Wolves."

"How about Miss Leon?"

"I told him I was just your graduate assistant," Miss Leon interrupted, "but I don't think he believes me."

"Green would naturally expect her to go along with us," McKee said. "That's what she gets paid for. To help."

He paused again, thinking of the sand on Canfield's lips and that something might go wrong with this plan.

"That sound all right?" he asked.

The Big Navajo moved his thumb absently back

and forth over his finger tips, studying McKee's face.

"Does Green have any schedule of where you're supposed to go next?"

"We didn't have any definite plans."

"Would Green be writing you anywhere? Anywhere set up to pick up letters?"

"Just Shoemaker's while we were here." He noticed Miss Leon was still looking at him and he felt himself flush. "We tell him where to forward to if we move. He'd get this letter from me saying where we were going and telling him to send our mail to the store at Mexican Water. It seems natural. You think he'd check on it?"

"Let's see how it looks on paper," the Navajo said.

McKee had been holding his right hand straight down. It had hurt, but the increased blood pressure should, he thought, build up the swelling. He raised it now, intending to feign pain. No pretense was necessary. The hurt was so far beyond what he had expected that his gasp was involuntary. He felt sweat on his face and nausea in his throat. When he finally rested his right forearm on the hood, he slumped against the truck, breathing hard, too dizzy to notice whether the Navajo had registered all this. I can't spoil this now, he thought. He has to believe I'm really trying.

"I'll start it, 'Dear Dr. Green,' " he said. His voice was thick.

He moved his right hand slowly and took the pen between his thumb and forefinger. In a moment he had one more gamble to make. He would suggest that he try to write the letter with his left hand, explaining to Dr. Green that he had injured his right one. He didn't think the big man would call this bluff. If the man was as smart as he seemed to be, he would see the objections. Green would wonder why Canfield hadn't written instead. And he would wonder why McKee wasn't coming in for medical attention. And the handwriting would be unidentifiable anyway— and that obviously was important. But, if he didn't see the objections, this whole desperate play for time might collapse.

He shifted the pen into the proper position, lowered the point and started the "D." The Navajo was watching him intently.

Again, a fresh wave of pain helped his performance. The flinch was completely involuntary, the spasm of a tortured nerve.

"Don't write it," Miss Leon said suddenly. "I don't trust him."

The Navajo turned toward her.

"Ellen," McKee said hurriedly, "if you had shown a little sense earlier we wouldn't be here. If you'd use what little brains you have, you'd see that this letter is our only way out of this mess. Now shut up."

He hoped, as he said it, that the anger would sound sincere to the Navajo and insincere to Miss Leon and thought bitterly that the reverse would probably be true. The hurt in Miss Leon's face looked genuine and the Navajo's expression was unreadable.

He tried again with the pen, finishing the "Dear" this time, and inspected the wavering scrawl with satisfaction.

"That's fairly close," he said. It looked nothing at all like his handwriting and the Navajo had plenty of samples in his field notes to make the comparison.

"It's not close enough," the Navajo said.

"How about writing it with my left hand?" McKee said suddenly. "We could say I'd hurt my right one." He tried to make his glance at the Indian seem natural, and held his breath.

"Dr. McKee. Think about it. That wouldn't look like your handwriting. If it doesn't look like your handwriting, it won't work no matter what you say." The Navajo was looking at McKee curiously. "Why would you write Dr. Green a lefthanded letter with Dr. Canfield around to write letters?"

"Just a thought," McKee mumbled.

The Navajo looked at his watch and then, for a long moment, at the man called Eddie. Eddie shrugged. "Whatever you think," he said. "I don't know the odds."

McKee was suddenly chillingly aware that his life was being decided. The Navajo looked at him, his face bland, with no trace of malice or anger. McKee was conscious of the ragged line rimming the iris of the Indian's eyes, of the blackness of the pupils; conscious that behind that blackness an intelligence was balancing whatever considerations it gave weight and deciding whether he would die.

"The hell of it is," the Big Navajo said, "we don't know how long we're stuck here."

"Whatever you think," Eddie said again. "Lot of money involved."

"Let's see that hand again," the Indian ordered.

McKee raised it slowly, palm upward, toward the Navajo.

He leaned slightly forward, scrutinizing the twisted finger. Like, McKee thought, a housewife inspecting a slightly off-color roast.

"Maybe soaking it will get that swelling down," the Indian said. "Soak it in hot water and get the swelling out. We'll take 'em up to the cliff place, Eddie."

From behind him, McKee heard a faint click. Eddie had slipped the safety catch on his automatic back into place.

"It's almost four o'clock," the Navajo said. "The hell of it is with this job we never know how much time we have."

longer sure of anything. This unexpected fact visible
at his feet fell like a stone in a reflecting pool, turning
the mirrored image into shattered confusion. The answer he had found converted itself into another question. Leaphorn no longer had any idea why Horseman
had died. He was, in fact, more baffled than ever.

Leaphorn had left the Chinle subagency at noon,
towing Sam George Takes's horse and trailer, deter-
mined to learn what the Big Navajo had been doing at
Ceniza Mesa. At first he drove faster than he should
because he was worried. Billy Nez had come home
from the Enemy Way, picked up his rifle, and left
again on his pony. Charley Tsosie, as usual, didn't
know where he had gone. But Leaphorn could guess.
And he didn't like the conclusion. He was sure Billy
Nez would ride to the place where Luis Horseman
had hidden. Nez would pick up the tracks of the Big
Navajo's Land-Rover there, and he would follow it.
Because Leaphorn couldn't think his way through
the puzzle of Luis Horseman's death, he had no idea
what Nez would find—if anything. And because
Leaphorn didn't know he worried.

Leaphorn began driving more slowly and worrying less as the carryall climbed the long slope past
Many Farms. He had been working his way methodically around the crucial question, the question which
held the key to this entire affair, the question of mo-

15

At approximately four o'clock Joe Leaphorn, sweating profusely, led his borrowed horse the last steep yards to the top of the ridge behind Ceniza Mesa. Almost immediately he found exactly what he had hoped to find. And when he found it the pieces of the puzzle locked neatly into place—confirming his meticulously logical conclusions. He knew why Luis Horseman had been killed. He knew, with equal certainty, that the Big Navajo had done the killing. The fact that he had no idea how he could prove it was not, for the moment, important.

At about ten minutes after four o'clock, Lieutenant Leaphorn found something he had not expected to find on the Ceniza ridge. And suddenly he was no

tive. By the time the carryall reached the summit of
the grade and began the gradual drop to Agua Sal
Wash the answer was taking shape. He pulled off the
asphalt, parked on the shoulder and sat, examining
his potential solution for flaws. He could find no serious ones, and that eliminated his worry about young
Nez. Nez almost certainly wouldn't find the Big Navajo on the Lukachukai plateau. The man would be
long gone. And, if he did find him, it wouldn't matter
much unless Nez did something remarkably foolish.

Leaphorn went through his solution again, looking
for a hole. The Big Navajo must have found the Army's
missing rocket on Ceniza Mesa.

Why, Leaphorn asked himself angrily, had he
been so quick to reject this idea when he learned the
reward was canceled? The Big Navajo had been clearing a track to the top when Billy Nez found him and
stole the hat. He would have needed such a road to
haul the remains down. And then he had cached the
rocket somewhere until he could find out how to collect the reward. Horseman had found the rocket and
claimed it. A Navajo would not kill for money, but
he would kill in anger. The two had fought—fought
in some sandy arroyo bottom. Horseman had been
smothered. And the Big Navajo had moved his body
down to Teastah Wash. Why? "To avoid having the
area where his rocket was hidden searched by Law

and Order people looking for Horseman." Now the
Big Navajo was waiting, with the inbred patience of
the Dinee, for the moment when sun, wind, and bird-
song made the time seem right to claim the Army's
$10,000. Or perhaps he had learned by now that the
reward had been canceled. It seemed to make little
difference. Leaphorn could think of no possible way
to connect the missile with the murder.

He looked out across the expanse of the Agua Sal
Valley, past Los Gigantes Buttes. There was Ceniza
Mesa—twenty miles away, a table-topped mass of
stone rising out of an ocean of ragged erosion like
an immense aircraft carrier. Eons ago the mesa had
been part of the Lukachukai plateau. It was still
moored to the mountain ramparts by a sway-backed
saddle ridge. It was on that saddle ridge that Billy
Nez had seen the Big Navajo working and it was there
Leaphorn would prove his theory. Perhaps Billy Nez
had lied. Leaphorn thought about it. Billy Nez hadn't
lied.

He pulled the carryall back on the pavement and
drove down the slope toward Round Rock, enjoying the beauty of the view. For the first time since
the body of Luis Horseman had been found he felt
at peace with himself. He switched on the radio. "Ha
at isshq nilj?" the broadcast voice demanded. "What
clan are you? Are you in the Jesus clan?" Navajo

with a Texas accent. A radio preacher from Gallup. Leaphorn pushed the button. Country music from Cortez. He snapped off the radio.

"He stirs, he stirs, he stirs, he stirs," Leaphorn sang.

"Among the lands of dawning, he stirs, he stirs.
The pollen of dawning, he stirs, he stirs.
Now in old age wandering, he stirs, he stirs.
Now on the trail of beauty, he stirs,
Talking God, he stirs. . . ."

The mood lasted past Round Rock, past the turn-off at Seklagaidesi, down eleven jolting miles of ungraded wagon track. Leaphorn still sang the endless ritual verses from the Night Way as he unloaded the horse where the track dead-ended at an abandoned death hogan. He trotted the animal across the broken, empty landscape, skirting Toh-Chin-Lini Butte, moving southeastward toward the Ceniza saddle. He saw the bones of a sheep, the empty burrows of a prairie-dog town, and the moving shadow of a Cooper's hawk swinging in the sky above him. He saw no tire tracks and he expected to see none. That would have been luck. Leaphorn never counted on luck. Instead he expected order—the natural sequence of behavior, the cause producing the natural effect, the human behaving in the way it was natural for him to behave. He counted on that and upon his own ability to sort out the chaos of observed facts and find in them this natural order. Leaphorn knew from experience that he was unusually adept at this. As a policeman, he found it to be a talent which saved him a great deal of labor. It was a talent which, when it worked unusually well, caused him a faint subconscious uneasiness, grating on his ingrained Navajo conviction that any emergence from the human norm was unnatural and—therefore—unhealthy. And it was a talent which caused him, when the facts refused to fall into the pattern demanded by nature and the Navajo Way, acute mental discomfort.

He had felt that discomfort ever since Horseman had turned up dead—contrary to nature and Leaphorn's logic—far from the place where nature and logic insisted he should be. But as he led his borrowed horse the last steep yards to the crest of the Ceniza saddle the discomfort was gone. The top of the ridge was narrow. In a very few moments he would find tire tracks and the tracks would match the tread pattern drawn for him by Billy Nez. Of that Leaphorn was certain. When he examined these tracks he would find the Land-Rover had driven up the saddle to the mesa top empty and had come down with a heavy weight on its rear tires. And then the irritatingly chaotic affair of Luis Horseman would be basically orderly, with only a few minor puzzles to solve.

The narrow ridge offered few choices of paths, even for a four-wheel-drive vehicle, and Leaphorn found the tire tracks quickly. There were four sets instead of the two he had expected to find, indicating two trips up and two trips down. He made no attempt to find meaning in that. He concentrated on the fresher tracks, establishing by the traction direction which of them had been made going up the slope. In an area where the soil was soft he checked the depth of the tire marks. Exactly as he had expected. On the trip down, the rear tires had cut almost a half-inch deeper.

Behind him the horse snorted and stamped, fighting off the flies.

"Horse," Leaphorn said, "it comes out just the way we figured it would."

Leaphorn rose from his squat and brushed a fly from the horse's back. There was no trace left of the nagging sense of wrongness and urgency that had dogged him for days, none of that vague, undefined feeling that something unnatural and evil was afoot in his territory. He understood now. It was a good feeling.

And then Lieutenant Joe Leaphorn took two short steps across the small place of soft, loamy earth and looked down at the older tracks. He recorded the fact that they had been dimmed by at least one rain shower. He noticed that this set, too, varied in the depth the rear tires had cut. It had taken, Leaphorn thought at first, two trips to haul down the remains of the shattered rocket. A split second later his mind processed what his eyes were seeing. On this round trip, the Land-Rover had carried its heavy load on the way up—not on the way down.

The Navajo language is too specific and precise to lend itself to effective profanity. Leaphorn cursed in Spanish and then—at length—in English.

It took Leaphorn almost three hours to piece together as much as he could of what had happened on this ridge and on the mesa to which it led. He worked methodically and carefully, resisting an urge to hurry. And when he put it all together, he had nothing but another enigma which offered no possibility of solution.

To Leaphorn's surprise the Land-Rover had approached the saddle from the southeast, emerging from the Chinle Desert from the direction of the Lukachukai ramparts. On the first trip up—perhaps as long as a month earlier—it had carried a heavy load over its rear axle. At several places the driver had stopped to cut brush out of the way, sometimes using an ax and sometimes a power chain saw. To traverse

the steepest slope, where the saddle rose sharply to
the lip of the mesa rimrock, he had used a winch line
in several places to help pull the vehicle up. Once on
top, the vehicle had driven fairly directly about a
mile across the mesa. There something heavy and
metallic had been unloaded on a flat outcropping of
sandstone, scoring the soft rock. From this point, the
Land-Rover had made a backing turn and driven directly back over the original track.

Even though the other tracks were weeks fresher,
he had spent most of the time sorting out the second trip. He finally concluded that on this trip the
Land-Rover had driven directly to the sandstone outcropping. Then it had returned to the rim where the
saddle joined the mesa. There several small trees had
been cut and a score of boulders moved, apparently to
clear a better roadway. At the site of this heavy work,
Leaphorn found the tracks of Billy Nez's rubber-soled
sneakers, marks of the Big Navajo's flat-heeled boots,
a bread wrapper, and an empty Vienna sausage can.
After Billy Nez had been here—and presumably after he had left with the Big Navajo's stolen hat—the
Land-Rover had driven back over the rim and back
to the sandstone. There the heavy object had been
reloaded and the Land-Rover had driven down off
the mesa. This much was clear. Leaphorn had found
three ponderosa poles used as a tripod, which must

have supported the pulley used to lift whatever it was the Big Navajo had unloaded and then reloaded.

Leaphorn rubbed his fingertips over his forehead, trying to re-create exactly what the Big Navajo had done on that second visit to the Ceniza Mesa.

He had first driven to the heavy object. And what then? Looked at it? Assured himself it was still there? Adjusted it? Fed it? Put fuel in it? Turned it off? Or on? No hope of guessing. And then the Big Navajo had driven back to the rim to improve the steep approach. Why? If he could winch the loaded Land-Rover up the slope he could winch it down, given enough time. Was that it? Time? Did he expect to be in a hurry coming down? Maybe, Leaphorn thought. Maybe that was it. Time. But Navajos didn't hurry. In fact, there was no word in the Navajo language for time.

And then the Big Navajo had discovered his hat had been stolen, had found the tracks of Billy Nez, and knew someone had watched him. Knowing this, he had driven back over the top, reloaded the heavy object, and hauled it down off the mesa. Why? Maybe because Billy Nez might find it. But where had the big man taken it? And what was it?

Leaphorn stood on the mesa rimrock and stared out across the Chinle at the Lukachukai slopes. The sun was down now. The tops of the evening thunderheads over the mountains were still a dazzling sunlit white, but below the fifteen thousand-foot level they turned abruptly dark blue with shadow of oncoming night. The desert was streaked with pink, red, and purple now, the reflected afterglow from cloud formations to the west. Normally Leaphorn would have been struck by the immensity of this beauty. Now he hardly noticed it. He stared at the darkening line of the Lukachukai ramparts, searching out the points of blackness, the open mouths of the canyons which drained it. Since the Land-Rover had come from the southeast, across the Chinle, it must have come from one of these. He could backtrack it. Twenty miles, he guessed. Maybe twenty-five, and a lot of it would be over bare slick rock. Even in daylight he wouldn't average a mile an hour. At night it would be impossible.

A burrowing owl, its wings stiff, planed up from the desert below him, banked into the invisible elevator of air rising up the mesa wall. It hung on the current a few feet below him—its yellow eyes examining the rimrock for incautious rodents feeding early. Leaphorn envied its mobility. Since the moment he had seen his orderly, logical explanation of Luis Horseman's death demolished by the hard facts of the Land-Rover's tire tracks, the old sense of urgency had returned. He had resisted it by sheer strength of will, forcing himself to concentrate on deciphering what had happened at this mesa. Now he resisted no longer. Instead, he thought about it—turning this itching impulse to hurry in his mind. What was it that bothered him?

He laughed, and the owl, making a second and slightly higher sweep over the mesa wall, panicked at the sound. It flapped past him, trailing its chittering *quick-quick-quick-quick* call, and vanished in the shadows.

Everything was bothering him, Leaphorn thought. Nothing fit. Everything was irrational. But why this sense of time running out, of something dangerous?

Leaphorn lit a cigarette and smoked it slowly, thinking hard. Luis Horseman had been killed. Billy Nez had found the tracks of the Big Navajo's Land-Rover near where Horseman had hidden. A Navajo had been killed and a Navajo had killed him—that was the presumption. Leaphorn studied this presumption, again seeking an answer to the central question. Why? Why did Navajos kill? Not as lightly as white men, because the Navajo Way made life the ultimate value and death unrelieved terror. Usually the motive for homicide on the Reservation was simple. Anger, or fear, or a mixture of both. Or a mixture of one with alcohol. Navajos did not kill with cold-blooded premeditation. Nor did they kill for profit. To do so violated the scale of values of The People. Beyond meeting simple immediate needs, the Navajo Way placed little worth on property. In fact, being richer than one's clansmen carried with it a social stigma. It was unnatural, and therefore suspicious. From far behind him on the mesa came the voice of the owl. *Ta-whoo*, it said. *Whoo*.

Where, then, was the motive? There was something about all this that seemed strangely un-Navajo. But the big man who drove the Land-Rover was one of The People. Leaphorn was sure of that, remembering the face in Shoemaker's. There had been times at first at Arizona State when Leaphorn had trouble with the faces of white men. He had noticed only the roundness of their eyes and their paleness, and all Belacani had looked alike to him. But he had no trouble with the faces of the Dinee. The Big Man had the face and the frame of a Tuba City Navajo—heavy-boned without the delicacy and softness added by the Pueblo blood mixture. And he wore braids. The trademark of the man who held to the Navajo Way. But why were the braids so short?

Leaphorn thought about that for a moment. And abruptly he again had an answer. Not all of it. But enough to make him urge the horse down the ridge-line much faster than the tired animal wanted to move. Enough to tell him that Billy Nez, hunting his witch in the Lukachukai canyons, might actually find one to his mortal danger. Enough to tell him that he must be at the hogan of Charley Tsosie at dawn. There he would pick up the boy's trail. The unshod horse should be easy to follow.

Mars rose over the black outline of Ton-Chin-Lini Butte as he loped across the Chinle breaks, his mood matching the gathering darkness. He was remembering his words to the Big Navajo at Shoemaker's—the casual words which he now was sure had caused Luis Horseman to die.

16

Bergen McKee had been dreaming. He stood detached from himself, watching his figure moving slowly across a frozen lake, knowing with the dreamer's omniscience that there was no water under the ice—only emptiness—and dreading the nightmare plunge which would inevitably come. And then the raucous cawing of the ravens mixed with the dream and broke it and suddenly he was awake.

He sat motionless for a second, perplexed by the dim light and the blank wall before him. Then full consciousness flooded back and with it the awareness that he was sitting, cold and stiff, on the dusty floor of a room in the Anasazi cliff dwelling.

McKee pushed his back up against the wall and looked at Ellen Leon, lying limply opposite him, face to the wall, breathing evenly in her sleep. He looked at his watch. It was almost five, which meant he had slept about six hours and that it would soon be full dawn on the mesa above the canyon. With that thought came a quick sense of urgency.

He looked at his hand, tightly wrapped now in bandage, and then glanced quickly around the room. The enclosure was much too large for living quarters. It had been built either as a communal meeting place for one of the Pueblo's warrior secret societies or as a storeroom for grain—three stone walls built out from the face of the cliff and, like the cliff, sloping slightly inward at the top. The only way out was the way they had come in—through a crawl hole in the roof where the wall joined the cliff. And there was no way to reach the hole without the ladder—the ladder which the Big Navajo had carefully withdrawn after leaving them here.

Outside, a raven cawed again and then there was silence. McKee leaned against the wall and tried to sort it out.

Whatever was happening here was the product of meticulous planning. That was clear. Behind the brush at the foot of the cliff there had been four sections of aluminum-alloy ladder. The man called Eddie had fit them quickly together, fastened them with bolts and wing nuts, and they reached exactly from a massive sandstone block at the top of the talus slope to this shelf. If the ladder was not custom-built for the purpose, at least the bolt holes had been drilled with this cliff dwelling in mind.

And, when they had reached the top, Eddie had pulled up the ladder, and laid it carefully out of sight. The action obviously had long since become habit. It would leave anyone passing below no hint that this cleft was occupied. It was equally obvious that the peculiar hideout had been occupied for weeks. Behind a screen of bushes which grew back from the ledge under the overhanging cliff there was all the equipment for a permanent camp—a two-burner kerosene stove, a half-dozen five-gallon cans, and a tarp stretched low to the ground protecting cartons and boxes. And there had been two bedrooms. Whoever else was involved must sleep somewhere else, perhaps directing this operation from somewhere outside. From what Eddie had said, others would tell them when they could leave.

And whoever they were, they had a radio transmitter. After Eddie had fished cans of meat and beans from under the tarp and fed them and started him soaking his hand in a pot of steaming water, the Big Navajo had climbed back down the ladder. He had sat for a long time in the Land-Rover and when he returned he had news.

McKee rubbed his knuckles across his forehead, remembering exactly. The big man had been grinning when he walked up to where Eddie was sitting— grinning broadly.

"Girlie says maybe tomorrow afternoon will do it," the Navajo had said. Eddie had looked pleased, but he had said something noncommittal. Something like Girlie's been wrong before. No. It was Girlie's been wrong three times, because the Indian had laughed then and said, "Fourth time's the charm for us." It had occurred to McKee then that if these men were leaving tomorrow they would no longer need a letter written by him. Once they had finished what they had come to do and had left this canyon why would it matter if someone came looking for Canfield and Miss Leon and himself? It would only matter that no one be left alive to describe them. Thinking that, he had decided to throw the water pot at the Big Navajo and jump Eddie, trying for Eddie's pistol. He hadn't thought he would get the pistol, but there would be nothing to lose in trying. And then the Navajo had baffled him again.

"Dr. McKee," he had said, "I think we'd better try to get that knuckle of yours back into joint, and tie it up with a splint. I'm going to be busy tomorrow, but by tomorrow night I'll want to get that writing done."

Thinking about it now, McKee was still puzzled. Eddie had carried a section of the ladder to the cliff ruin and they had climbed against the overhang to the top of this wall . . . and then down into the pitch darkness of this room. The Navajo had told him to sit on the floor and hold out his hand. He had argued with the Indian that the joint was broken, not just dislocated.

The Navajo had laughed. "They feel like that when they're pulled out, but we can get it back in the socket."

The big man had squatted beside him, with Eddie holding the flashlight from above, and had taken McKee's swollen right hand in both of his own, and suddenly there had been pain beyond endurance. When he had returned to awareness, Miss Leon was holding his head and his hand was tightly wrapped. He had been sick then, violently sick, and then they had talked.

"Where did they go?" McKee had asked. It was almost totally dark in the windowless room, with only a small spot of moonlight reflecting through the roof hole relieving the blackness.

"I heard them a little while ago," Miss Leon had said. "I think they were both out there where their sleeping rolls are. And then I heard what sounded like the ladder being moved."

"I guess they climbed down," McKee said.

There was a long silence. McKee felt her shoe against his leg. The touch seemed somehow personal, and intimate, and comforting.

"Dr. McKee." Her voice was very small. "I didn't hear all of what you and that Navajo said when we were at Dr. Canfield's camper. Dr. Canfield's body was in there, wasn't it? He killed Dr. Canfield?"

"Yes," McKee said. There was no use trying to lie to her. "I guess he did."

"Then he'll kill us, too," she said.

"No," McKee said. "We'll find a way out." He could think of no possible way.

"There isn't any way out," Miss Leon said. "It would take a magician to get out of this."

McKee was glad it was dark. Judging from the sound of her voice, she was on the ragged edge of tears.

"I didn't have a chance to tell you," he said. "We think maybe that electrical engineer you were looking for may be working somewhere way up the canyon."

"Jim? Did you find him?"

"Some Indians saw a van truck driving up in here. Do you know if he was pulling a generator?"

"There was a little trailer behind his truck," she said. "Would that be a generator?"

"Probably," McKee said. He searched his mind for some way to keep this conversation going, to keep her from thinking of sudden death.

"I noticed your ring, Miss Leon. Is this Dr. Hall—er, Jim—the one you're engaged to?"

"Why don't you call me Ellen?" she said. There was a pause. "Yes, I was going to marry him."

McKee noticed the past tense instantly. And then it occurred to him why she used it. She thought she would soon be dead.

"What's he like?" McKee asked. "Tell me about him."

"He's tall," she said. "And rather slim. Blond hair, blue eyes. He's very handsome really. And he's—he's, well—sometimes moody. And sometimes very happy. And always very smart."

The voice stopped. I match none of that, McKee thought, except the moody part.

"He graduated magna cum laude." The voice paused, then continued, "And our society doesn't have the proper respect for magna cum laude."

"I guess not," McKee said.

Ellen laughed. "I was quoting Jim," she said. "Jim is—well, Jim is very ambitious. He wants things. He wants a lot of things, and he's very, very smart—and—and so he'll get them."

"I don't know why," McKee said. "But I guess I

never was very ambitious." He wished instantly that he hadn't said it. It sounded self-pitying.

"What else about him?" McKee asked. He didn't enjoy hearing her talk about the man. But it was better for her to talk, better than having her sitting silent in the dark—dreading tomorrow. She talked rapidly now, sounding sometimes as if she had waited a long time for someone to listen, and sometimes as if she was talking only to herself, trying to understand the tale she was telling.

She had met Jim at Pennsylvania State on the first day of a Shakespeare's Tragedies class. He had taken the chair to her left and she had hardly noticed him until the professor called the roll. But the professor's voice had risen slightly in a question as he read "Jimmy Willie Hall" off the class card. The professor had intended no rudeness and he made this clear by nodding in acknowledgment to Jim's "Heah," but someone in the back of the room had sniggered and this churlishness to a stranger had embarrassed Ellen, embarrassed her all the more because she, too, had smiled at the ludicrous sound. She had glanced at the young man with the outlandish name and noticed he wore cowboy boots and had a wide-brimmed gray felt hat pushed under his chair. On a campus where styles were set by the casual, careless conformity of young men from Philadelphia one was as out of place as the other. And, when she had looked at him again, she had seen that while his face, neck, and hands were incredibly sunburned, his forearms about the wrists were as white as the shirt he was wearing.

"He looked very strange and out of place," Ellen said. And suddenly she laughed. "I thought he would be lonely," she said, sounding incredulous.

She had spoken to this Jimmy Willie Hall in the lecture building hallway. Jim had said, in reply to her comment that he wasn't from the East, that he was from Hall, New Mexico, and when she had asked where that was, he had said he wasn't really from Hall, exactly, because their place was twenty-one miles northwest of there, in the foothills of the Oscura Mountains. It was just that they picked up their mail at Hall. He guessed he should say he was from Corona, which was larger and slightly closer.

The conversation had been inane and pointless, Ellen recalled, as exploratory chats with strangers tend to be. She asked why, if Corona was larger and nearer, they picked up their mail at Hall, and he had explained that there was no road from the Hall ranch to Corona. To get there you had to go through the Oscura Range and Jicarilla Apache Reservation or over the malpais—across seven miles of broken lava country. You can't even get a horse over that, he had explained. The only time he had tried, his horse had broken a leg and he had been bitten by a rattlesnake.

"That sounds like he was trying to impress me," she said. "But he wasn't. A girl can tell about that. He was just telling me about a silly mistake he had made." Ellen's voice stopped. "I guess I knew right then he wasn't lonely," she continued, thoughtfully, "and that I had never seen anyone like him."

He had seemed, she remembered, like someone visiting from the far side of the globe her father kept in the office of his pharmacy—someone completely foreign to all she knew. As different from the men she had dated as his empty Oscura foothills were from her family's elm-shaded residential street in a Phila-delphia suburb.

"You remember *Othello?*" Ellen asked suddenly.

"*Othello?*" McKee said, surprised.

"Yes. The Moor of Venice. We studied it that se-mester, after *Hamlet.* You remember how Desdemona was fascinated by Othello?"

"I remember," McKee said, trying to remember.

"That was us," Ellen said. "That was our private joke.

"Remember how it goes?" She paused a moment.

"'A maiden never bold;
Of spirit so still and quiet that her motion

Blush'd at herself; and she—in spite of nature,
Of years, of country, credit, everything—
To fall in love with what she fear'd to look on!
It is a judgment maim'd and most imper-
fect . . .'"

"Yes," said McKee, "I remember it." He felt immensely sad.

"I would say that," Ellen said, "and Jim would say Othello's lines:

'It was my hint to speak—such was the process;
And of the Cannibals that each other eat,
The Anthropophagi, and men whose heads
Do grow beneath their shoulders. This to hear
Would Desdemona seriously incline. . . .'"

Ellen stopped again. And when she continued the voice was shaky.

"'I loved him for the dangers he had passed.
And he loved me that I did pity them.'"

McKee reached across the darkness and found her hand. "It's going to be all right," he said. "We'll get out of here and find him."

"Can't you understand?" she asked, and her voice

sounded angry now. "Why should I pity someone like Jim Hall? Why should anyone pity anybody who has everything?"

McKee couldn't think of an answer.

"Because he doesn't know he has everything?" Ellen suggested. "Because he isn't happy?

"Sometimes he is, but mostly he isn't. He's angry. He says he's caught in a system which keeps you on the treadmill. Forty years on the treadmill, he says. He talks about it a lot, about how it takes a million dollars to beat the system, to pay your own ransom, to buy back your own life."

She laughed again, a bitter sound. "I guess he . . . Well, I guess Jim will make a million dollars," she said.

"Not teaching on an engineering faculty," McKee said.

"Oh, he's not going to do that," she said. "He's going with one of the electronic communications products companies and he's bringing along one of his patents, so it's a very good job."

"Is that what he's working on out here?" McKee asked. "Trying it out."

"Oh, no. This is another one, I think. I—well, I wish I understood it better. Something to do with very narrow-range sound transmission. He explained it to me—quite often—but I don't really understand it."

McKee started to ask her why she was looking for Dr. Hall and bit back the question. The answer was obvious, and none of his business. A woman who loves a man would simply want to see him.

"Dr. Canfield was nice, he was nice, a nice man," Ellen said. "But he was too polite to ask why I was chasing after Jim. And you've been nice, too. But would you like to know?"

"It's your private business," McKee said. "No, I don't want to know."

"I want to tell you. I have to tell someone," she said. "I came because I wanted to tell Jim—to tell him that I think he's wrong, and he's going to have to make a choice. He's got to quit wanting a million dollars. He has to. I've come all the way out here. He has to understand."

It sounded utterly feminine to McKee, the reverse side of Sara's logic, and a simpler assignment. A brilliant, ambitious man could easily enough fail to make a fortune. But how could a Bergen McKee, a natural on the treadmill, make himself rich?

And, thinking that, McKee, after forty hours without rest, was suddenly asleep.

Now he was fully awake again. He pushed himself to his feet and surveyed the room. The floor was covered with a heavy deposit of dust. He could feel it, flourlike, under the soles of his shoes. But the condition of the room was surprising. It was virtually intact. The roof sagged only at one corner, where the ceiling beams had snapped with rot, and plaster still clung to most of the lower portion of the walls.

McKee flaked off a section of plaster with his thumbnail, broke it and examined it. Inside it was almost black—a mixture of animal blood and caliche clay used by the pueblo-building people. It was stone-hard and would last for centuries and so would the cedar poles in the roof when protected from weather under a cliff. But not for this many centuries. Left alone, the roof would have crumbled long ago and the top of the walls would have fallen inward. This ruin must have been partially rebuilt—restored by one of the later Pueblo people who used the canyon before the Navajos arrived and drove them out.

It was then he saw the face. He stood for a moment staring at it, putting together what it meant, feeling a sense of excitement building within him. The face was drawn on the plaster in something yellow—probably ocher. It was faded now and partly missing where chips of plaster had fallen away. A roundish outline with a topknot, long ears, and a collar. The figure was unquestionably a Hopi Kachina—either the Dung Carrier or the Mud Head Clown. And below it to the right were two more stylized outlines.

From the Hopi mythology McKee recognized Chowilawu, the spirit of Terrible Power, with four black-tipped feathers rising vertically from his squarish head and a horizontal band of red blinding his eyes. The third head had been almost erased by flaking. Only the dim outline of a protruding ear and the double vertical cheek stripes signifying a warrior spirit remained. Down the wall there were other markings—the zigzag of lightning, bird tracks, the stair-stepped triangles of clouds, and a row of phallic symbols. Undoubtedly, one of the Hopi clans had used this as a ceremonial kiva.

He stood absolutely silent a moment, thinking, and then squatted beside Miss Leon and put his hand on her shoulder.

"Time to wake up."

She rubbed her arm across her eyes.

"Very domestic," McKee said.

She looked up at him and then pushed herself up against the wall, trying to straighten her tousled hair with her fingers. "Oh. What time is it?"

"About four forty-five," McKee said. "We shouldn't have wasted all that time. We need to get out of here."

"Out of here? But I don't see how we can." Miss Leon looked up at the exit hole in the roof and then at McKee. "What do you mean? How can we?"

"The Hopis lived in this. They rebuilt it. Have you read anything about how the Hopis build their pueblos?" It occurred to McKee as he said it that he was showing off and the thought embarrassed him. Ellen looked puzzled.

"They always built an escape hatch at the bottom of a wall," he explained. "A hole into the next room, and then they would fill it in with rocks that could be easily pulled out. Kept them from being penned up in part of the structure if they were under attack."

"Oh," Ellen said. "You think there's a way out, then."

"I think so. We can find out. It would be in one of the inside corners."

And most likely, McKee thought, in the corner adjoining the cliff. Bracing over the escape hole would have been easier there.

The corner was littered with broken cedar sticks. Above, occasional moisture seeping down the cliff face had accelerated the slow work of decay. The builders had cut holes into the soft stone to support the ends of ceiling beams and here the rot had started first.

McKee selected one of the sticks and began pushing the debris away from the corner. He worked carefully, trying to avoid noise. But the powdery dust rose in a cloud around him. Ellen knelt beside him, pushing the dust back carefully with her hands.

"Don't make any noise."

"Do you have any idea what this is all about?" she whispered. "Why does he want you to write that letter?"

"I don't know what's going on," McKee said. "Maybe they're crazy."

"I think you know about the letter," Miss Leon said. She stopped digging and looked at him. Her face was chalky with dust. White and strained. McKee looked away.

"He explained why he wanted the letter," McKee said.

"And if you believed him, you would have written it," Ellen said. She sat back on her heels, still looking at him. "Why don't you stop treating me like a child? You know as well as I do that if they were going to turn us loose they wouldn't need the letter."

"O.K.," McKee said. "I think you're right. They want the letter because they know that someday there's going to be a search started for us and they don't want the search to be in here. They don't want the search to be in this canyon ever—or at least not for a long, long time."

"But why not? Do you know why?"

"No," McKee said. "Can't even make a good guess at it. But it has to be right."

He leaned back against the cliff and wiped the dust off his face.

"I didn't think so at first. I thought that, whatever they were doing here, it was making them wait for something, and they didn't know how long the wait would be, so they didn't want interference. But that's not right, because it seems to be happening today. They could just leave us here, and it would be a long time before anyone found us. A lot more time than they would need to get away."

"That's what I thought of, too," Ellen said.

"Did you notice how they camped?" McKee asked. "No garbage hole. Put all the cans and stuff in gunny sacks. And Eddie, when he lit the stove, he put the burned match in his vest pocket."

"I didn't notice. I guess I didn't think of that."

"When they pull out of here there won't be any traces left. Not after the August rainy season, anyway. Unless there was some reason for a search, no one could ever know anyone had been in here."

Beneath the pile of debris in the corner, the plaster looked almost new. He jabbed it with his stick and cursed inwardly when the rotten wood snapped. For this he needed his pocket knife and the Big Navajo had taken it when he had searched him. Or had he?

McKee suddenly was aware of the weight of the knife in his shirt pocket. He had dropped it there with his cigarette pack when he hurried from their tent—hands full of odds and ends—in his futile race to escape. It was a ridiculous place to carry a pocket knife, and the Navajo had overlooked it.

McKee fished it out and pulled open the blade—noticing he could hold it between the thumb and forefinger of his right hand with little pain. With the knuckle back in joint the swelling must be going down. There would be no chance now of persuading the Navajo that he couldn't write.

The plaster chipped away in sections, revealing a rough surface of stone with mud mortar chinking. A moment later a yard-square sheet crumbled and McKee saw he had guessed right. The fitted stonework ended in a crude half-arch in the corner two feet above the floor. The first stone he pulled on was jammed tightly, but the second slipped out easily.

McKee rocked back on his heels, looking at the stone. It was about the size of a grapefruit and felt clumsy in his left hand. He tried to shift it to the right, but it fell into the dust.

Miss Leon looked at the stone and then at him.

"I think we can get out," he said. "We can if the room on the other side hasn't fallen in and buried this crawl hole under a lot of big rocks."

"What do we do if we get out?" Her voice was very small.

"Did you hear them come back during the night?" McKee said.

"No. I didn't hear anything. But we don't even know if they left. Maybe just one climbed down."

"The Big Navajo said he had to leave," McKee said. "And he said he might not be back until tonight. If Eddie didn't stay up here on the ledge, we'll try to find a way off."

Miss Leon looked skeptical.

"Come on," McKee said. "The Hopis lived here long enough to rebuild part of this place and they didn't like being in places where they could be boxed in. There's a good enough chance that they had some sort of escape route off the cliff. They always had a hidden way out if they could."

There was another alternative. If they found no way off the cliff, he could try to keep Eddie and the Indian from climbing back up. He might surprise them, catch them on the ladder—defenseless from a rock dropped from above. With surprise it might work. But there was a rifle in the Land-Rover. They would be good with it—probably very good.

"But what if Eddie stayed up here?" Ellen said. "I'll bet he did."

"I don't know," McKee said. "Just let's hope he didn't."

He tried to make his grin reassuring without much success. He was thinking of the way Eddie handled the pistol. For the first time it occurred to him exactly what his problem might be. He might have to find a way to kill a man. He turned away from the thought.

Outside the hole he stood tensely, listening. The ravens had flown away now and the only sound was the morning wind and the faint whistling of a horned lark on the canyon rim high above him. The Hopis had repaired this room, too. He could tell from the remnants of plaster. But a slab of stone had fallen from the cliff, crashing through the roof and tumbling much of the east wall outward. Denied this support and protection, the roof had collapsed and centuries of wind had drifted a hump of sand and dust against what remained of the wall. Over this hump, McKee surveyed what he could see of the east end of the ruins.

The shelf gradually narrowed to the east. From what he remembered seeing yesterday from the canyon bottom, this entire east end was filled with ruined walls, ending just short of the point where a structural fault split the canyon wall from floor to rim. That would be the place to look for an escape route. That narrow chimney would be the only possible way up. The thought of it made his stomach knot. As a graduate student, he had climbed down such a slot to reach a cliff house at Mesa Verde, and the memory of it was an unpleasant mixture of fear and vertigo.

He climbed cautiously over the rubble of the exterior wall at the edge of the shelf and looked down into the canyon. The Land-Rover was not in sight. That should mean the Navajo had not returned from wherever his business had taken him. Nor was there any sign of Eddie. That meant nothing. Eddie might be sleeping below him in any of a thousand invisible places. Or Eddie might be only a few yards away on the cliff.

Here the Anasazis had crowded their building almost to the edge of the cliff, leaving along the lip of the precipice a narrow walkway, which was now buried under debris. McKee moved along it gingerly, keeping as close as the fallen rocks would allow to the wall of the storeroom. At the corner, behind a water-starved growth of juniper, he stopped.

When he looked around the corner, Eddie would be standing there. Eddie would have the pistol in his hand and would—without any change of expression—shoot him in the head. McKee thought about it for a moment. Eddie might look faintly apologetic, as he had when he had introduced himself at the Land-Rover. But he would pull the trigger.

McKee stood with his back pressed against the stones and looked out across the canyon. It was almost full dawn now. Light from the sun, barely below the horizon, reflected a reddish light from a cloud formation somewhere to the east onto the tops of the opposite cliffs. A Piñon jay exploded out of a juniper across the canyon in a flurry of black and white. He heard the ravens again, far up the canyon now. It was a beautiful morning.

McKee leaned forward and looked around the wall.

Eddie was not in sight. The stretched tarp was there, and the stove, and other equipment. Both sleeping bags were gone. So was the ladder. McKee felt himself relaxing. Eddie must have climbed down and left them alone on the shelf.

McKee was suddenly aware that he would be plainly visible from below. He moved back behind the juniper and stood, thinking it through. He glanced at his watch. Five A.M. Then he heard Eddie whistling.

Eddie walked around the jumble of fallen rock at the west end of the shelf, not fifty feet away. He was carrying his bedroll under his right arm and his coat slung over his left shoulder—whistling something that sounded familiar. He dumped the bedroll, folded the coat neatly across an outcrop of sandstone, and squatted beside the stove.

McKee stared numbly through the juniper. Of course the Big Navajo had left nothing at all to luck. He had taken the ladder but left the guard behind.

Eddie was combing his hair. His shoulder holster, with the pistol in it, was strapped over his vest. About twenty yards away, McKee guessed. He could cover maybe ten yards before Eddie saw him, and another five before Eddie could get the pistol out, and then Eddie would shoot him as many times as were necessary.

The first plan McKee considered as he worked his way slowly back along the cliff edge involved waiting in ambush at the corner of the storeroom until Eddie mounted the ladder to bring them their breakfast. He imagined himself sprinting the fifteen feet before Eddie, encumbered with food, could draw the pistol, knocking the ladder from under him and triumphantly disarming him.

It might work—if Eddie brought them breakfast. There was no reason to believe he would. Much more likely he would first check on his prisoners with pistol in hand.

The second plan, even more fleeting, involved having Miss Leon raise a clamor—perhaps shouting that he was sick. This would probably bring Eddie up the ladder to look in the hole in the storehouse roof. But he would come cautiously and suspiciously. The third plan survived a little longer because—if it worked—it did not involve facing Eddie's pistol. He and Miss Leon would work their way—unmissed and unheard—to the east end of the shelf. There they would find the Hopi escape route in the chimney and would climb to freedom. It was a pleasant idea and utterly impractical. It was far from likely that Ellen could make the climb and impossible for anyone to make it without noise. McKee considered for a moment how it would feel to be hanging on hand-holds a hundred feet up the chimney with Eddie standing below aiming at him. He hurriedly considered other possibilities.

One involved finding a hiding place back in the ruins and waiting in ambush, rock in hand, for Eddie to come hunting for him. The flaw in this one was easy to see. There would be no reason for Eddie to hunt. He would simply wait for the Navajo to return, believing there was no way off the cliff.

It would be necessary to make Eddie come after him.

McKee dropped on his stomach at the crawl hole.

"I'm right here," Ellen whispered. "I heard him whistling. Did he see you?"

"No," McKee said. "He's cooking breakfast."

"You know what," Ellen said. "I said it would take a magician to get out of this room. You're a magician."

"Um-m. Look—make sure your watch is wound," McKee said. "I want you to wait thirty minutes and then come out here and make some sort of noise. Knock a rock off the wall or something to attract him. But don't run. Don't give him any reason to shoot."

"What are you going to do?" Her whisper was so faint he could hardly hear it.

"Remember. When he comes, give up right away.

Put your hands up. And tell him I'm climbing up the escapeway back where the cliff is split at the east end of the ruins. Tell him I'm going for the police."

"Is there really a place you can climb out?"

"I don't know yet," McKee said. "The idea is to get the jump on him."

"There isn't any place. He's going to kill you." She made it a flat statement.

If Ellen said anything else, McKee didn't hear it.

"Ellen," he whispered. "Do you understand what to do?"

"Yes. I guess I do. But is thirty minutes enough?"

McKee thought about it. Every minute that passed might bring Eddie checking. Or it might bring the Big Navajo back. He was suddenly acutely conscious that he was probably setting the time limit on his life.

"I think thirty minutes," he said.

It was eight minutes more than Eddie allowed him.

It had taken very little time to defeat his hopes that the ruins would offer a point of ambush. Along the narrow pathway which followed the lip of the shelf, the walls were too crumbled to provide a place of concealment from which he could attack. Under the cliff itself the ruins were better preserved—some still standing in two stories—but they offered only a hiding place, no place from which to launch an attack. At the end of the shelf, where a massive geologic fault had shifted the earth's crust eons ago and split the cliff, there was no effective cover at all. McKee edged his way carefully past the dwelling's final crumbled corner.

Here the path was buried under tumbled stones. A misstep meant a plunge into the crevasse left by the fault.

McKee looked at his watch. He had used thirteen minutes and accomplished nothing. Here at its mouth the crevasse was about fifteen feet across. Beyond it the shelf continued. It was slightly lower and after a few yards tapered away to nothing.

From where he stood it was impossible to see what the crevasse in the cliff offered. The Anasazis had built their structure to the very base of the cliff wall. The exterior wall had fallen outward over the precipice, but the spreading limbs of piñon screened the narrow opening.

He moved carefully over what remained of partition walls, pausing once to look down into the crack. The split was sheer, and although the narrow slot was partly filled with broken slabs of rock flaked off the walls above, it was much too far to jump.

McKee hurt his hand again climbing what remained of the back wall. He had forgotten the finger for a moment in the overpowering need to know if the crevasse held some possibility for him, and had shifted his weight to it. He was still sick with the pain when he lowered himself into the darkness behind the wall. A minute ticked away as he sat in the dust, holding his hand stiffly in front of him, letting the throbbing diminish and his eyes adjust to the darkness. What he saw both disappointed and encouraged him.

There was no natural pathway into the crevasse as he had hoped. The shelf did not extend into it. But the Anasazis had cut foot and hand holds into the sandstone, making it possible for a person to work his way back into the slot. Somewhere back in the darkness where the crack narrowed, where a man could brace himself between the opposing walls, there would be a way to the top. If he could dispose of Eddie, he could make it. But what about Eddie?

McKee studied his position. There were two ways into this dark cul-de-sac where he now sat between wall and crevasse—over the crumbled wall as he had come, or by pushing past the out-thrusting branches of the piñon. Eddie would probably come over the wall for exactly the same reason he had done so. The piñon had angled outward toward the sunlight. One could force his way past it, but bending by the heavy branches would require a tightrope walk along the very lip of the crevasse. Not knowing where McKee would be, Eddie wasn't likely to risk that. He would choose the wall.

McKee thought about it. If Eddie came over the wall fast—moving from the bright morning light on the shelf into this darkness—then there would be a chance. But that wasn't likely to happen. Eddie would be taking no risks. He would climb the tumbled rocks of the wall slowly, pistol ready. He would pause at the top, studying the gloom. And, if he did, McKee would be a mouse in a trap.

He tested the extending main branch of the pi-ñon. If he could pull it back enough and tie it to some-thing, the route past the tree would be inviting. He could use his shirt as a rope, and tie one end well out on the branch. By putting his full weight against it, he could bend the tree well back from the lip of the cliff—opening an easy walkway. But where could he tie it?

A second after the ideas came to him, he heard Ellen.

Her voice was high, almost hysterical. He heard Eddie, an angry sound, and Ellen again—shouting now. And then the shot. A single crack of noise which released a rumble of echoes to bounce up and down the canyon.

"And now she is dead," McKee thought. "Canfield is dead and she is dead."

He bit the corner of the khaki shirt collar between

his front teeth, pulled it taut with his left hand and
split it gingerly with the knife. The pain was there
when he held the knife, but he could tolerate it. He
ripped the shirt down the back, twisted the two sections, and knotted them to his makeshift rope. Then
he pulled out his belt and looped it around an outcrop of stone beside the wall.

Now it would reach. He pulled against the tree,
thinking numbly that Eddie had not given him thirty
minutes and that Ellen had chosen to shout a warning
in the face of Eddie's pistol. He strained against the
rope of shirt, pulled it through the looped belt, and
wrapped it twice. His right hand was no help with
this heavy work and he used his teeth to pull the knot
tight. In a moment he would confront Eddie.

He was almost ready. He laid the knife on a rock
protruding from the wall, sorted through stones in
the dust at his feet and chose one which fit well in
his left hand. In a very few minutes it would be over.
Eddie would come. If Eddie walked past the tree, he
would cut the shirt and the limb would slash at Eddie. And, as he cut the rope, he would come over the
wall with the rock. If Eddie had been blinded by the
whipping limb, or hurt, or even confused, he would
kill Eddie. Either way, it would be over then. McKee
thought of that. It was better than thinking of Ellen's
voice and the sound of the pistol.

Eddie came almost too soon. McKee settled himself high on the rubble and looked over the top and Eddie was there. He was standing on the pathway at the corner, where the shelf was cut by the crevasse, studying the ruins. McKee shrank back behind the screen of piñon limbs as Eddie turned toward him. The gunman's vest was unbuttoned now and he held the pistol in his right hand, close to the body. The barrel, McKee noticed, always pointed with his eyes, like the flashlight of a man searching in the dark.

McKee felt a pressure in his chest and became aware he was holding his breath. He released it and gripped the rock.

Eddie moved now. He walked directly along the edge of the crevasse, just as McKee had done, stepping carefully over the tumbled partition walls. Twenty feet away he stopped and stood in a half crouch, studying the tree and the wall.

"McKee," he said, "I had to shoot your woman." Eddie's tone was conversational. He stood for a moment listening—no more than the polite pause for reply.

"Killing you is going to cost me thirty thousand dollars," Eddie said. "It's going to cost George twice that much." He paused again. "Are you going to make me do it?"

McKee found he was holding his breath again. Eddie was examining the wall, making his choice.

McKee looked at the rock in his hand. He turned his body, braced himself, and threw it in a high arching toss up the crevasse. There was a sudden echoing clatter as the stone bounced from wall to wall. Eddie took five quick, almost running, steps down the path and then stopped abruptly just short of the piñon.

McKee held the knife blade against the taut cloth. Eddie looked up along the wall and then squatted, peering past the lower branches of the piñon, so close now that McKee could only see his left shoulder and part of his back.

It happened very quickly then.

Eddie moved swiftly into the gap between tree and crevasse and McKee slashed downward with the knife. He knew even as the rope parted that Eddie had stopped again. He had underestimated the gunman's caution.

Coming over the wall, McKee saw only part of what happened. There was the blast of Eddie's pistol, fired into the swinging mass of the limb. Then the blond man, with lightning reflexes, leaped backward in a spinning crouch—swinging the pistol barrel toward him.

Eddie, suddenly, was no longer there. There was a

cry—a sound mixed of surprise and anger and fear—
and a crashing thump. Eddie's reflexive leap had carried him off the edge of the cliff into the crevasse.

When McKee first looked into the crevasse he
presumed Eddie was dead. The man had apparently
struck a sloping slab of sandstone about twenty feet
below the shelf, bounced from that against a block-
shaped mass of black rock, which jammed the center
of the crack, and then fallen another ten feet. He was
caught in an awkward jackknifed sitting position between rocks about fifteen feet above the sandy floor
of the crevasse. Eddie's pistol lay on the sand, about
forty-five feet down. McKee stared at it longingly. It
was as unreachable as the moon.

And then he saw Eddie's head move. Eddie was
looking up at him. His nose was bleeding, McKee
noticed, and he was breathing through his mouth.
McKee stared at the man, feeling a mixture of embarrassment and pity.

"I fell off," Eddie said.

"Yeh," McKee said. "When you jumped back from
that tree."

He started to say he was sorry, but caught himself.

"Can you get down here to me? I got to have help."

"I don't know," McKee said. "George took the ladder down. You know any other way?"

"I was going to draw forty-five thousand dollars," Eddie said. "They had it written up so I'd get fifteen thousand when they were finished and then thirty thousand if nobody knew about it a year from now. That's why we had to have you write that letter."

The blood from Eddie's nose ran across his chin. He coughed. "I can't feel anything in my arms."

"Who are they?" McKee asked. "What are you doing in here?"

"George was getting more because he made the contract and it was up to him," Eddie said. "After this one, if we got it all, I'd of had almost two hundred thousand dollars saved up." He coughed again. "You don't pay taxes on it."

Eddie's head tilted forward. He seemed to be staring at the rock in front of him. McKee knew he was looking at death. If Eddie had been Navajo, soon his ghost would have been escaping to wander eternally, combining all that was weak, and evil, and unnatural in the man, and leaving behind all that was natural and good. Only the Dinee who died before their first cry at birth, or of a natural old age, escaped this fate and enjoyed simple oblivion. Eddie's ghost would be a greedy one, McKee thought, always coveting material possessions—the Navajo ultimate of unnatural wickedness.

Eddie coughed.

"Eddie, where's George now? How long will it be before he comes back?"

It took Eddie a moment to raise his head. "Today's when they were trying to get it finished. George had to go out and uncover the sets and after that . . ." Eddie paused to cough again. "Then we were going to pull out of here. One more day for George to clean up and then we'd be finished."

"But when will George be back?"

"I—I don't know," Eddie said.

"Please," McKee said. "I have to know."

"No. It wouldn't help. He works out of Los Angeles, but I heard about him all the way back East. They say he never broke a contract." Eddie coughed again. "Never screwed up a job. He'll kill you and your woman and then he'll go on away."

McKee felt a sudden surge of hope. It lasted only a second.

"Didn't you kill her?"

"Oh," Eddie said. His voice was weak. "I forgot for a minute."

He peered up at McKee, frowning. "Told her not to yell," he said. "Maybe it didn't kill her."

McKee left him talking. He ran, hurdling the crumbled walls, back to where Ellen would be.

She was lying almost out of the crawl hole. She had apparently been emerging on hands and knees when Eddie shot her. McKee stood a long moment looking at her, feeling infinitely lonely and terribly tired. It wasn't until he lifted her that he realized she was still alive.

The bullet had cut through her cheek, deflected past her jawbone, struck the top of her shoulder, and torn out through the back of her shirt. McKee brought water, canned food, the first-aid kit, and one of the sleeping bags from the campsite. He laid her on the bedroll and examined the wounds. The slug apparently had hit her right shoulder blade, breaking it. It had deflected out through the back muscle, leaving a hole around which a seep of blood was beginning to clot. He rinsed the wounds, powdered them with disinfectant from the kit, bandaged her face, and applied a pad of gauze to the ragged tear where the bullet had finally emerged.

There was nothing else to do. He trotted back to the crevasse. Maybe Eddie could tell him something useful. Eddie was still staring at the rock in front of him, but now Eddie would answer no more questions.

McKee stared down at the body, thinking of what the blond man had told him. The Big Navajo was from Los Angeles. Probably, McKee thought, a "Relocation Navajo"—a child of one of those unfortunate families moved off the drought-stricken Reservation to urban centers during the 1930's. It had been one of the most disastrous experiments of the Bureau of Indian Affairs, turning hungry sheepherders into hungry city alcoholics. If George had been raised in Los Angeles, it would explain his weak command of the Navajo gutturals, and why what he knew of witches came from books. And maybe it would explain an Indian with the underworld connections which Eddie had seemed to imply. But it didn't explain why George and Eddie had been assigned to scare sheepherders out of this canyon country. Or why it was so important that no one learned they had been here.

The metal of Eddie's pistol reflected the early-morning sun. With that, McKee thought, he could simply wait for the Big Navajo to return, shoot him, carry Ellen down the ladder and take her to the hospital in the Land-Rover. But the pistol was beyond recovery. No way down into the crevasse and no way up if he got down.

He thought about it. Without the pistol he could probably keep the Big Navajo off the cliff. There were food and water at the camp. He could wait the big man out. But Ellen would be dying.

McKee chewed on his lip, trying desperately to think of the best solution. It was then he remembered the truck. Old Woman Gray Rocks had said it was parked in Hard Goods Canyon, nine miles up from the mouth of Many Ruins. That must be close—within two miles at the most. He made his decision.

It took him only a few minutes to hide Ellen Leon where the Big Navajo might not be able to find her. He carried her on the sleeping bag back into the ruins under the cliff. He put her in a room, with food and water beside her, and readjusted the bandage on her face. He saw then that her eyes were open.

"Bergen." She held out her hand and he took it—conscious of how small and fragile it felt.

"Lie very still," he said. "I'm going to climb out and get help."

"Bergen," she said again. "Be careful."

He ran back to the fissure in the cliff. He would climb out and find the truck. Somehow he would find the truck. If he didn't it would take a day and a night to walk to Shoemaker's. Eighteen or twenty hours, he guessed, which was about twelve more than he could spare.

He pushed past the piñon tree into the dark fissure, swallowing his dread of the climb. She had said Hall was smart—brilliant. If he could find Jim Hall, maybe Hall would be smart enough to save the girl he was engaged to marry.

17

The sun was almost directly overhead when McKee found the wires. He squatted in the thin shade of a juniper and examined them—a cable about the diameter of his finger paralleled by a lighter wire. Both were heavily insulated with gray rubber, almost invisible on the rocky ground. The heavier one, McKee thought, would carry electrical current. The lighter one might be anything, maybe even a telephone wire. They must be part of the data-collection system for Dr. Hall's sound experiments, McKee knew, and they gave him the second hope he had felt since emerging from the chimney three hours earlier.

The first had come an hour ago when he had seen the boy on the horse. He had stopped to catch

his breath and make sure of his directions on the plateau. He had glanced behind him, and the boy had
been there—not two hundred yards away—silently
staring at him. The boy was wearing what looked
like a red cap. But, when McKee had waved and
shouted, the horse and rider had simply disappeared.
They had vanished so suddenly that McKee almost
doubted his eyes.

"He knows he's in witch country," McKee thought,
"and he's spooky." Trying to follow him would be a
foredoomed waste of time.

Following the wires, on the other hand, would be
simple. At one end there would be some sort of gadget
of the sort which concern electrical engineers. At the
other end—with any luck at all—he would find the
engineer. And Hall would have a truck and maybe a
radio transmitter. The cable ran southeast across the
plateau toward the Kam Bimghi Valley and northwest
back toward the branch canyon McKee had been skirting. It was an easy choice. McKee trotted toward the
canyon, following the cable.

At the rim, the cable looped downward, disap-
pearing under brush and reappearing where it was
strung across rocky outcrops. McKee paused at the
rim, staring up the canyon after the cable.

This branch canyon was much shallower than
Many Ruins and its broken walls offered several

fairly easy ways down. From the canyon floor, McKee heard an echoing ping, ping, ping—the sound of metal striking metal. A flood of elation erased his weariness. Hall's truck must be there, and Hall with it. And it wasn't more than a quarter of a mile away.

The pain came with absolutely no warning, just as he took a step down off the rimrock. Behind the pain, perhaps a second, he was conscious of the flat snap of a rifle fired a long way off. Then he was conscious only that he was falling and of suffocation— or a terrible need to draw a breath into lungs that wouldn't work. He was on his back now, on a pile of talus just under the rim. The sky in front of his eyes was dark blue. He could breathe again, although inhaling hurt. And he could think again. He put his hand where the pain was, on his right chest. It came away hot and red. Someone had shot him. Who? The boy on the horse? That made no sense. The Big Navajo. Yes, of course.

McKee pushed himself into a sitting position against the rimrock and gingerly examined the damage. He could feel the bullet hole on his back—a small burning spot. It had come out left of his left nipple, tearing a hole through which blood now welled. Broken ribs, he thought, but the lung must have been missed. It still inflated.

McKee coughed and flinched at the knife in his

ribs. He tried to think. The Big Navajo must have returned to the cliff, and had found Ellen. No use thinking about it.

From up canyon he heard the dim, puttering sound of a two-cycle engine. Probably a generator motor. And probably down in the canyon bottom Hall hadn't heard the shot. Or if he had heard it would have no reason to be warned by it. He had to reach Hall in time to tell him.

McKee pulled himself to his feet, took three steps along the talus and stopped, gasping, supporting himself by hanging on to the rubber-clad cable strung across the rocks. It would take him half an hour at this rate to reach the truck. And he didn't think he had that much time.

Over the rim he could see nothing at first. An expanse of plateau, sparse clumps of buffalo grass, a scattering of drought-dwarfed piñon, juniper, and creosote bush, a stony surface on which nothing moved. Then he saw, to his left, the figure of a man. The man walked slowly, a rifle with a telescopic sight held across his chest. He moved unhurriedly, relentlessly, inexorably toward the point of rimrock from which McKee had fallen. Five hundred yards away, walking almost casually toward him under a broad-brimmed black hat, was certain death.

McKee fought down a desperate impulse to run.

When he conquered the panic he found it replaced by a hard, cold, overpowering anger. He looked around for a weapon and became abruptly conscious of the soft rubber insulation of the cable gripped in his palm.

You son of a bitch. You bastard. You won't just finish me off like a crippled animal. You'll have to come and get me.

Had the Big Navajo been careless, had he simply walked his slow walk directly to the rimrock, McKee would have run out of time. But the Big Navajo took no chances at all. When McKee finally heard his boots, the sound came from below. The hunter was stalking cautiously, skirting the point on the rim where he must have seen McKee knocked down by his bullet, taking his time.

McKee had worked feverishly. He pulled the slack cable over a boulder and slammed it twice with a rock. The cable severed and the end sprang away in a shower of sparks. He stripped five feet of the thick rubber tubing from the dead end with his pocket knife. While he worked, the plan formed in his mind. Just up the canyon, a huge ponderosa had fallen against the rocky cliff—a dead log half obscured by a thick growth of pine saplings. He would crawl into that darkness, tie the rubber to two sapling trunks to make a catapult, cut himself a lance from another sapling, and hope the Big Navajo made a mistake.

The Big Navajo was making no mistakes. McKee could see him now, moving in a half-crouch ten yards below the rimrock. The big man stared upward at the place where McKee's blood smeared the boulder. McKee could see his profile, shaded under the broad rim of the new black hat. It was a handsome face, hawklike and intent. The Big Navajo moved up to the boulder and knelt beside it. He examined the bloody talus debris and then stood, scanned the slope below, and began walking carefully along the route McKee had taken.

McKee pushed his heels deeper into the pine needles and tested his lance against the tension of the rubber. He had cut a yard-long length of a three-quarter-inch pine stem, given it a crude point, and then hammered the punch tool of his knife into the soft wood six inches from the heavy end. Snapped off, this prong of steel provided the hook on which he had caught the rubber.

He was lying almost flat, his weight pulling against the tough rubber. Down the shaft of the sapling, he saw the Navajo's hat rise into view as he moved slowly up the slope. Then his shoulders, then his belt. The man stopped. He looked at the fallen tree, at the growth of young ponderosa. He stared intently from the sunlight into the deep shadows.

McKee held his breath, fought against the dizziness. Four or five steps closer, he prayed. Keep coming. Keep coming.

The Navajo stood, staring directly at him. His face was thoughtful. Suddenly he smiled.

"Well," he said. "There you are."

It seemed to McKee to take quite a little time. The Big Navajo's right hand brought the rifle butt smoothly up to the right shoulder, the left hand swung the barrel toward him, the Navajo's face moved slightly to the right, behind the telescopic sight. All this while McKee was releasing the lance.

Most likely the telescope made the difference. Over open sights, the Indian would have seen the lance at the moment of its launch, seen it soon enough to simply step aside. Behind the sight, he saw it too late. There was a sound—which McKee would remember—something like a hammer striking a melon. And the clatter of the rifle falling on the rocks. And the sound of the Big Navajo tumbling backward down the slope.

McKee crawled out of the thicket and picked up the rifle. It seemed incredibly heavy. The Big Navajo had slid, head downward, between two boulders. McKee looked at the man and hastily looked away. The pine shaft had struck him low on the chest. There was no chance at all that he was alive. The black hat lay by the boulder, the sun reflecting off the rich silver of its concho band. And up the slope was a furry bundle tied with a leather thong. McKee untied the thong. A wolf skin unrolled itself.

McKee felt a whirling dizziness. *Always wanted a witch's skin. Hang it on my office wall. Maybe give it to Canfield.*

He remembered, then, that Canfield was dead, and was conscious that his side was wet and his pant leg was sticking to his thigh. He put the wolf skin over his arm and started down the slope toward the canyon floor. He fell once. But he remembered Ellen Leon and got back to his feet. And finally he was on the sandy canyon floor, where walking was easy.

"Put down the rifle."

"What?" McKee said. A boy was standing behind a clump of willows. There was a horse by him, the reins dragging.

"Put down the rifle." The boy had on a red baseball cap and he had a short-barreled rifle in his hands. An old .30–30. It was pointed at McKee.

McKee dropped the Big Navajo's rifle. The wolf skin fell with it, dropping in a folded hump on the sand.

"Where's the other witch?"

"What?" McKee said. It was important to think about this. "He's dead," he said, after a moment. "He shot me and I killed him. Back up there under the rim-rock." McKee pushed the wolf skin with his toes. "This is his witch skin," he said, speaking now in Navajo. "I am not a witch. I am one who teaches in school."

The boy was looking at him, his face expression-less.

"There is a truck a little ways up here," McKee said. "You must let me get to that truck and the man there will help me."

"All right." The boy hesitated, thinking. "You walk. I will walk behind you."

He was within thirty yards of the truck before he saw it—parked in a thicket of tamarisk and willow just off the canyon floor. Beside it a gasoline generator was running. The back door of the van stood open, a padlock dangling in the hasp. Through the doorway McKee heard the faint sound of someone whistling and then of metal tapping on metal.

McKee stopped.

"Hello," he shouted. It didn't sound like his voice.

McKee took two more steps toward the truck, conscious the whistling had stopped.

A man appeared in the doorway of the van, blond, in a denim jacket, taller than McKee and younger, with a hearing aid behind his left ear. His blue eyes rested for a second on McKee, registering surprise and shock.

"What the hell happened?" he said. And then he was out of the truck, coming toward McKee.

"Got shot," McKee said. "Somebody shot me." His voice sounded thick. "Get the bleeding stopped." He sat down abruptly on the sand.

The blond man was saying something.

"Don't talk," McKee said. "Listen. Are you Jim Hall?"

"How did you know that?"

"Listen," McKee said. "Tell this boy here that I'm not a witch and he will help you." He paused now and started again, trying to pronounce the words.

"Ellen Leon was shot, too. Ellen Leon. She's up at that big cliff dwelling in a canyon. . . ." McKee tried to think. "In that canyon that runs into Many Ruins south and west of here."

The man was squatting beside McKee now, his face close. McKee had trouble focusing on the face. The face was surprised, amazed, excited, maybe frightened.

"You said Ellen?" the man said. "What the devil is she doing out here? What happened to her?"

"Man shot her. Needs help." McKee said. "Go help her."

"Who shot her?" the man asked.

"Man named Eddie." McKee said. He was very tired. Why didn't this fool go? "Don't worry," he said, "Eddie's dead now." He heard the man asking him something but he couldn't think of an answer. And then the man's hands were on his face, the man was talking right into his face.

"Listen. Tell me. What happened to Eddie? What happened to Eddie? And was there a man with him? Where's the man who was with him?"

McKee couldn't think of how to answer. Something was wrong.

He tried to say, "Dead," but Jim Hall was talking again.

"Answer me, damn you," Hall said, his voice fierce. "Do the police know about this? Has anybody told the police?"

McKee thought he would answer in a moment. Now he was concentrating on not falling over on his side.

Hall stood up. He was talking to the boy with the red baseball cap, and then the boy was talking. McKee could hear part of it.

"Did you see the witch he killed?"

He couldn't hear what the boy answered.

"You were right when you guessed that," Hall was saying. "This man here is a Navajo Wolf. Give me your rifle."

McKee stopped listening. He was asking himself how Jim Hall knew about the man with Eddie, asking himself why Hall was acting the way he was acting. Almost immediately, with sick, despairing clarity, he saw the answer. Hall was the Big Navajo's other man.

The boy hadn't given Hall the rifle. He was standing there, looking doubtful.

"Put the rifle in the truck then," Hall said. "We'll leave the witch here. Tie him up first. And then we'll drive to Chinle and tell the police about him." Hall paused. "Hand me the rifle and I'll put it in the truck."

"Don't," McKee said. "Don't give him the rifle."

Hall turned to look at him. McKee focused on the face. It looked angry. And then it didn't look angry anymore. Another voice had said something, something in Navajo.

It said, "That's right, Billy Nez, don't give him your rifle." And the anger left Jim Hall's face as McKee looked at it, and it looked shocked and sick. Then it was gone.

McKee gave up. He fell over on his side. Much better.

The metallic sound of the door in the van slamming and then a voice, the voice of Joe Leaphorn, and a little later a single loud pop.

I can't faint now, McKee told himself, because I have to tell him about Ellen. But he fainted.

18

He was aware first of the vague sick smell of ether, of the feel of hospital sheets, of the cast on his chest, and of the splint bandaged tightly on his right hand. The room was dark. There was the shape of a man standing looking out the window into the sunlight. The man was Joe Leaphorn.

"Did you find her?" McKee asked.

"Sure," Leaphorn said. He sat beside the bed. "We found her before we found you, as a matter of fact." He interrupted McKee's question. "She's right down the hall. Broken cheekbone and a broken shoulder and some lost blood."

He looked down at McKee, grinning. "They had to put about ten gallons in you. You were dry."

"She's going to be all right?"

"She's already all right. You've been in here two days."

McKee thought for a while.

"Her boyfriend," he said. "How'd it all come out in the canyon?"

"Son of a bitch shot himself," Leaphorn said. "Walked right away from me into the truck, and slammed the door and locked it and got out a little .22 he had in there and shot himself right through the forehead." Leaphorn's expression was sour. "Walked right in with me just standing there," he added. He didn't sound like he could make himself believe it.

McKee felt sick. Maybe it was the ether.

"You've got more Navajo blood in you now than I do," Leaphorn said. "The doc said you had a busted oil pan. Took ten gallons."

"I guess you had to tell her about Hall."

"She knows."

"He must have been crazy," McKee said.

"Crazy to get rich," Leaphorn said. "You call it ambition. Sometimes we call it witchcraft. You remember the Origin Myth, when First Woman sent the Heron diving back into the Fourth World to get the witchcraft bundle. She told him to swim down and bring back 'the way to make money.'"

"Knock off the philosophy," McKee said. "What happened? How did you find her?"

"I've noticed this before," Leaphorn said. "Belacani women are smarter than you Belacani men. Miss Leon got herself over to that camp stove on that cliff. She poured out the kerosene and made herself a smoky little smudge fire. You could see it for miles."

He grinned at McKee.

"Something else she figured out that you might like to know about. She was having her doubts about Hall when I got there. All excited. Said you'd gone to find him and she was afraid something might happen to you. Miss Leon wanted me to climb up that split in the cliff and go chasing across that plateau to rescue you."

McKee felt better. He was, in fact, feeling wonderful.

"Why didn't you think of something simple, like making a big smoke?" Leaphorn asked. "Climbing up that crack in the rock was showing off."

"How was I going to know you'd be wandering around out there?" McKee asked. "It's supposed to be the cavalry that arrives in the nick of time, not the blanket-ass Indians."

McKee had a sobering thought. "I guess you know I killed those two men?"

"Not officially, you didn't," Leaphorn said. "Officially, we've got just two dead people. Officially, Dr. Canfield and Jim Hall were killed in a truck accident. Miss Leon and you were hurt in the crash. And officially Eddie Poher and George Jackson never existed."

"Was that their names? And what was going on in there, anyway? What was Hall doing?"

"It's a secret," Leaphorn said.

"Like hell it's a secret," McKee said. "If you want me to tell some phony story about Canfield getting killed in a truck wreck, you don't have secrets."

"I'm not really supposed to know all of it myself."

"But you do," McKee said.

Leaphorn looked at him a long moment.

"Well," he said. "You cut one of his cables so I guess you know Hall had portable radar sets staked out on that plateau. And you know that plateau is under the route from the Tonepah Range up in Utah down to White Sands Proving Grounds."

"Yeah," McKee said. "I knew that much." He wondered why he hadn't thought of radar.

"Hall was sitting with his radar right under what the military calls its 'Bird Path,' and when the birds flew from Tonepah the radar was feeding information into a computer in the van. Hall was putting it into tapes."

"What were they testing?"

"The military intelligence people don't tell a Navajo cop things like that."

"I'll bet you can guess."

Leaphorn looked at him again. "Maybe the MIRV. The Multiple Intercontinental Re-entry Vehicle. Read about it in *Newsweek*. One missile, but it drops off five or six warheads and some decoys. I'd guess that if I was guessing."

"It still doesn't make sense. What was he doing with the information and how'd a guy like Hall get tied up with that bunch?"

"If you'll shut up and listen, I'll tell you."

From what they now knew, Leaphorn explained, Hall, Poher, and Jackson had arrived on the Reservation separately almost two months ago. A fingerprint check had been enlightening. Poher was relatively unknown. One arrest on suspicion of conspiracy to rob a bank, some East Coast Mafia associations, but no convictions. Jackson was another story. He was also known as Amos Raven, and Big Raven and George Thomas, with a long and violent juvenile record dating back into the late thirties in Los Angeles, and one adult conviction for armed robbery, and a half-dozen arrests for questioning in an assortment of crimes of violence—all Mafia-connected.

"A Relocation Indian. Jackson seems to have been born in Los Angeles." Leaphorn laughed. "California Navajo. That's what had me hung up. I was expecting him to act like The People and all he knew about The People he must have got out of a book."

"*Case Studies in Navajo Ethnic Aberrations*, for one," McKee said, "by John Greersen."

"Anyway," Leaphorn continued, "Jackson had apparently been picked for this assignment simply because he was a Navajo and looked like one. His job must have been to help Hall set up his equipment and make sure that nobody knew what was going on. It wouldn't have seemed difficult, for the very reason the military chose this route for its overland missile. The country was almost completely deserted. Hall set up in Many Ruins Canyon complex, which The People avoid because of the Anasazi ghosts, and Jackson scared the few stragglers out by pretending to be a witch."

"Except Horseman," McKee said.

"Yeah. Except Horseman." Leaphorn's voice was flat.

"It wasn't your fault," McKee said.

"Remember what I said to Jackson at the trading post? I said if Horseman don't come out we'll come in looking for him. So Jackson brought him out for us and laid him out where we couldn't miss him."

"Use your head, Joe. There was no way you could have stopped it from happening."

"I was slow figuring it out," Leaphorn said. "I smelled something about Jackson. But I figured him to act like a Navajo and he was acting like a white man."

"Thanks a lot," McKee said.

"If he was a Navajo, no matter what he was doing in there, killing Horseman would have screwed it up for him. He would have gone off somewhere and had a sweat bath, and then he would have found himself a Singer and got himself cured and forgot about it."

Leaphorn told McKee about the Enemy Way and about finding the place where Jackson had built the road up Ceniza Mesa.

"He had put one of the radar sets up there and then he was improving his road so he could get it down fast, without using the winch. When he missed his hat, he knew someone had seen him, so he moved the radar back over to the plateau. I didn't know about the radar but it was beginning to be clear by then that there had to be a lot of money involved somewhere. You put it together—a lot of money and a killing. It's not natural, and it's not Navajo."

"All right," McKee said. "I'll buy that. But how did Hall get into it?"

"I don't know," Leaphorn said. "I hear the federals are looking into a little West Coast electronics company with Mafia ownership. I think Hall did some work for them before—something legitimate." He looked at McKee pensively. "Didn't that business about Jackson wanting you to write the letter tell you something?"

"It told me he didn't want anybody coming in there looking for us," McKee said. "What else?"

"Think about it," Leaphorn said. "If you have a bunch of computer tapes giving you the exact performance of the other guy's ballistic missile system, it's worth a bunch of money. But it's worth a lot more if the other side doesn't suspect you've got it. Right?"

"Because if he suspects he changes the system," McKee said. "Eddie said something about that. About the letter being worth a lot of money."

A nurse came in then, a Navajo girl, in the uniform of the Indian Service Hospital. She scolded Leaphorn for staying too long, took McKee's temperature and gave him a capsule and a drink of water.

When McKee awoke again, there was a tray beside his bed with a covered dish of food on it, and beside the dish was an envelope.

He turned the envelope in his good hand, aware before he opened it of the familiar feeling of his common sense struggling with his perennial incurable optimism. The note inside was from Ellen Leon. Tomorrow, it began, the doctor would let her come to visit him. It was not just fourteen blunt words in blue ink on blue paper. It was a long letter.

About the Author

TONY HILLERMAN was the president of the Mystery Writers of America and received the Edgar and Grand Master awards. His other honors include the Center for the American Indian's Ambassador Award, the Spur Award for Best Western Novel, and the Navajo Tribal Council's Special Friends of the Dinch Award. He lived with his wife in Albuquerque, New Mexico.

"Must-read mysteries, thrilling new look!"

The Redbreast	*Careless in Red*	*Death at La Fenice*	*The Blessing Way*
Jo Nesbø	Elizabeth George	Donna Leon	Tony Hillerman

OLIVE EDITIONS for $10 EACH

Available for a Limited Time Only

	The Mapping of Love and Death	*A Darker Domain*	*Gaudy Night*
Moriarty			
Anthony Horowitz	Jacqueline Winspear	Val McDermid	Dorothy L. Sayers